MARCO?

Marco?

—

Kalman Dean-Richards

LENDAL PRESS

First published in 2022 by Lendal Press
Woodend, The Crescent, Scarborough, YO11 2PW
an imprint of Valley Press · lendalpress.com

ISBN 978-1-912436-76-7
Catalogue no. LP0010

Copyright © Kalman Dean-Richards 2022
All rights reserved.

The right of Kalman Dean-Richards to be identified as the
author of this work has been asserted in accordance
with the Copyright, Designs and Patents Act 1988.

A CIP record is available from the British Library.

Cover and text design by Peter Barnfather
Cover painting by Tony Chenery
Edited by Paige Henderson and Seline Layla Duzenli

Printed and bound in Great Britain
by Clays Ltd, Elcograf S.p.A.

For my dad, who picks up the pieces.

One for sorrow,
Two for joy,
Three for a girl,
Four for a boy,
Five for silver,
Six for gold,
Seven for a secret,
Never to be told.
Eight for a wish,
Nine for a kiss,
Ten for a bird
You must not miss.

1. The Madman and The Magpie

I'd been alone for three months, and now I was really seeing things. Things like the solidarity of the house cats in their hostility towards strays. Like the accelerated yellowing of the appliances in the kitchen. Sarah had been right.

Maybe two months? Hard to say.

I was on my way to her sister's house because that was where she was supposed to be, and I was driving too fast and everyone else was driving too slow. Old men in flat caps, buses to nowhere. Dawdling. Considered recycling a roadside bouquet to make myself look less spontaneous, but the tulips had gone crisp and there was a discoloured teddy bear noosed to the stems that I didn't have time to untie. Took a shortcut through a red light and grazed a lollipop man in a clown costume. Nothing could stop me.

It was like things had been getting clearer and clearer and I'd just needed something to snap me into action, and now I'd finally snapped.

I'd been napping in the afternoon, riding out a migraine a dozen paracetamol hadn't killed, and I'd heard him in the living room.

Stripped off the duvet, put my slippers on.

Clack Clack Clack – sound came again – metal, like an axe against the TV stand, calling me out.

Stepped over the floorboards that creaked, made it to the door and squatted against it. Heard him drop something on the laminate and spin around in gritted boots to pick it up.

Then nothing.

Then *Clack Clack Clack*.

Squatting nude, the brown light in the bedroom made me look like a madman in the full-length mirror on the wardrobe door. He'd opened a window in there too, and my nipples clenched at the cold so I reached up and took my dressing gown from the hook above me, pulled it on.

So I looked less mad –

Clack Clack Clack.

– and it occurred maybe that wasn't the impression you wanted to give. What if *he* was mad? Breaking into a home with the resident napping inside, calling them out by bashing an axe against the furniture…it suggested a degree of instability. Maybe I had to meet him on his own terms. *I* could be a *violent nut* for all he knew. Even madmen are wary of violent nuts.

When they promoted Jim Stant over me, Sarah said I was asleep at the wheel –

Clack Clack Clack.

– when Stant started laying people off and made me go first, she said 'Do something Marco. Rattle the cage.'

I was shaking. With rage, maybe. A violent nut. Snarled in the mirror, gaunt, sweating in the cold.

Rattle the cage.

Clack Clack Clack.

I listened for his movements. Slow, confident footsteps. Oblivious? Uncaring.

I'd make him care.

Stamp on his throat. Hang him in the bike shed. Get Sarah back.

Clack Clack Clack.

The air was damp and my lungs couldn't handle a full breath, so I didn't breathe. I straightened up against the door and the adrenaline hit my shins and everything trembled.

Rattle the cage.

Clack.

Clack.

Clack—

I ripped through the door and into him, crouched in the corner with a hammer, pulling wires through the skirting boards. *My* skirting boards. My robe blew open in the wind he'd let in and I let it billow. He twisted around, looked at me and then over my shoulder, but the doorway was mine.

'Oh, sorry to wake you,' he said. 'Should be done in a minute or two.'

I put my hand on his collar and pulled him tight, and he smiled at me like I was everyone's cunt.

I hit him in the smile and he went down and dropped the hammer, and I picked him up and hit him again. He came at me like I always knew he would: fierce, bald, chiselled, but I was the madman. Struck me that there was something familiar about his face, but there wasn't time to ask – his hands came at me like to gouge my eyes and I buried a slipper in his stomach before he got the chance. I was quick, powerful. He reached for the hammer but I was too fast across the floor, and then it was in my hand. Tried to reason with me next, crawling backwards towards the clothes-horse in the opposite corner, around the settee, but the blood in his mouth garbled his words and I wasn't listening anyway. Nothing to be said. I looked at the hammer and back to him.

'Rattle the cage.' I said, banged it against the radiator behind me.

Clang Clang Clang.

'You think I won't do it?'

Clang Clang Clang.

And *CRASH*, as the King magpie from number twenty's conker tree flew at full speed into the open window pane and flopped down two floors into the downstairs garden. Seeing his opportunity, he lifted himself up against the wall and launched the clothes-horse – clothes that had been hanging for weeks, boxers that were inexplicably still moist. Forced a barrier between us that let him stumble down the stairs and through the front door.

I didn't chase him. I went to the bedroom and watched him run, hunched over and coughing and spitting, throw himself into a van that backfired and fishtailed into a telephone pole, and disappeared into its own diesel cloud.

Down in the back garden the ginger stray sat in the pushchair and looked quizzically at its tail, ignorant of the new chew-toy hidden in the grass in front of it. The magpie twitched its wings and wondered where it had all gone wrong.

I closed the window and wondered the same thing.

2. The Sister

Wired. I considered a hot drink before leaving the house but I hadn't wanted to lose the buzz so I just had the milk from the morning's bran flakes, which turned out to be the milk from much older bran flakes.

I felt like walking over. I felt like running over but that seemed like it'd come across impulsive and I didn't want to come across impulsive. I jogged to Syn – what we called the car – gave the driver-side door a couple of goes before it dawned on me someone had smacked the back door and the front into an unopenable wall. There wasn't a mechanic in the Black Country I didn't owe money. I let it go, got in the passenger side.

In front of me Mrs Brian's ragdoll kitten mounted her C-Class and started rimming itself. I let that go too. I was the bigger man. For now.

When I pulled away there was somebody shouting in the crescent behind me, and I wondered if it was about my car but I didn't have time to find out – I was racing: barking at flat-caps, throwing it blind around buses. Skipping gears, picking teeth, looking for sunglasses in the glovebox and finding them a lens light in the footwell.

I'd been daydreaming and everyone else was on the move. Daydreamed to thirty. Daydreamed out of work, out of a tenancy agreement, out of love. Daydreamed into a hammer fight and made it out alive.

Now I was awake, alert. And I had a plan that was thin on detail, thick on conviction: get Sarah back. Rattle the cage.

I met Sarah through work when we were both twenty-three. The first time we spoke she said I made her laugh, and I spent the next six years trying to live up to that.

Her parents had moved to Switzerland when she was nineteen, left her a two-bed apartment in the city to share with her obnoxious older sister. She wanted out, wanted to move to the sea, drink wine and sell rabbits out of a beach hut. I liked the sound of it, didn't know how it was done.

I said she should move in with me, and she said it made sense.

Lucy, Sarah's sister, lived in the next town. She'd sold the apartment, had a house with three floors and a perfect invisible husband who paid for endless redecoration. She looked like her mother never kissed her, and you couldn't blame the woman.

At Lucy's wedding, she told Sarah she wished *she* could find someone like what'shisname. Propositioned some groomsmen. Sarah told her 'Not everyone believes in Mr Right,' but Lucy didn't believe anything anyone else said, lined her up an afternoon tea with a heart surgeon, who swore to me over scones he'd had no idea.

Sarah didn't need Mr Right, but she needed me to be able to afford the rent. I'd have to get the old house back.

That was essential. Settle up with the landlord about the wallpaper stains in the second bedroom. Get a job so we could afford a holiday. She wanted to take me to Paris, but I never had the money or I didn't want to spend it. That's where we'd go. I could learn the language, propose to her in a patisserie with a ring in a chocolate eclair. It was coming together. I could see the French applauding.

First, for the second time, I had to free her from Lucy.

The road was empty so I parked in front of next-door's drive, slid over and let myself out, tied my gown. I'd been there a handful of times, and since the last they'd had new windows with those metal diamonds wankers liked, and a pickle green paint job.

I shut the smaller gate behind me, knocked.

The venetian blind in a top window looked like it shook and settled. No answer. I knocked again, and when I did the latest in their fleet of Land Rovers rumbled around the corner like a guard-dog and stood still in front of the main iron gate. The engine clicked off and I looked at it and it looked at me. Out came Lucy, shaking her head, with her hair down around her face in a commendable effort to conceal as much of it as possible. I rolled up the sleeve of my right arm but it fell back down. She made the hop from vehicle to pavement and her ankles held firm.

'Yes, I suspected you'd be around eventually.' We looked at one another through the black bars. Her voice made my teeth grind. 'Although even I didn't think you'd take three months.'

'Where's Sarah?'

'Been smoking marijuana today, have we?' She talked like a school teacher keeping you at lunch. I didn't answer. 'If you wouldn't mind removing yourself—'

'I'm not going anywhere.'

'From the flower bed...' She looked down at my feet and laughed the way you do when something's not funny. I twisted on the heels of my slippers, stepped out.

'Where is she, Lucy?'

She pursed her lips and looked over my head at the house, but there was no-one at the windows still, and no-one at the door.

'Look at you, Marc. I mean do you really think she wants to have any sort of conversation with a...' she paused for effect 'man...who leaves his flat in a dressing gown?' I didn't look at me because I knew how much it'd turn her on if I did. 'I mean, what *have* you done to your vehicle?' Didn't surprise me she'd noticed the scrape – picking flaws and stating the obvious her favourite pastimes. 'T-t-t-t.' She shook her head slow, like a doctor who'd just gassed Grandma. 'I think she'd prefer that you leave.'

'I'm not asking you.'

'Oh, you haven't come around to break into my house again, have you?'

Me and Sarah simultaneously misplaced our house-keys around Christmas 2015. They kept a spare but told us they were away for the weekend when I'd called. I was half-way through the bathroom window when the truth came out and the lights came on.

'She'll want to talk to me. Where is she?' Now she looked at me like the hammer guy had.

She sighed.

'I don't know, Marc.' Rolled her eyes.

'What do you mean you don't know?'

'Look, it's not for you to know where Sarah is. She's... gone.'

'Gone?'

'She won't be answering your calls.'

I stepped back into the freesias. Gone?

'Gone for how long? Gone where?'

'Months! At least a month. While you were in your pit. Could be anywhere – she's a free woman. Look never mind that – Sarah can look after herself Marc. Perhaps you should learn how to do the same.'

'You don't know where she is?'

'...'

'Have you reported her missing?'

'Reported...Marc, look, I'm getting the impression that you're still in a vulnerable state—'

'Vulnerable? Sarah's vulnerable. Your sister's fucking vulnerable.'

Mystified by the notion of concern.

I walked the path and she watched me with a dumb expression.

'Marc...' she said.

I tried the driver door and then went around and got in, dialled her mobile and it answered before it even rang.

'Sarah...'

Nothing. Breathing. A landline ringing in the distance. Then nothing again.

'Where are you?'

It was in my head. This stifled, uncomfortable sound. Or I wanted it to be. But it came and came again. Crackled down the earpiece. Laughter. Then unrestrained. Sincere, ugly laughter. And a sniff. And silence.

'Don't call here again,' he said, and the line went dead.

I called again.

'Hellooo this is Sarah. I'm not in the mood to answer the phone, but if you leave a message I'll dismiss the notification and cross my fingers you call back another time.' I waited for the beep, then I hung up.

Lucy scrolled through her phone as though her eyes weren't on me. I took off the sunglass, ran my finger through a stick of rainbow light the chip in the windscreen sometimes made. And then I stole my focus back.

3. The Money

The petrol light flickered on and off, then on again.

I swirled it around – Lucy, the laugh. Tried to rewind the voice, probe it, but the shock was distorting and all I could hear was myself. 'Don't call here again.' Don't fucking tell me not to call again I'll call who I fucking want.

Finished the argument, pulled a U-turn, lost the back end and rerouted a campervan through the new bike lane on the Oldon Road. Nobody's fault.

The plan was still simple – still had to rattle the cage, still had to get Sarah back. Just now I had to find her before I could do it.

Finding her was gonna take petrol, and now they'd fixed the CCTV at Texaco petrol was gonna cost money. The last of the dole had gone to BT for a broadband call-out I was still waiting on, the banks wouldn't look at me, so there was only one way I was getting that.

Tommy Gigger always had money – in the cushions, in sealed bags in the top of the toilet, notes tucked behind radiators, wrapped around U-bends. He knew where every penny was, and I never saw him spend a thing. At school they said he'd killed his own dad over a twenty pound note. That was untrue, of course, because Tommy's dad had died in a high-speed police chase on his son's fifteenth birthday. I'd been a pallbearer at the funeral.

Now, he lived at home and cared for his sick mom, smoked weed relentlessly.

He looked around the net curtain and smiled at me. Hugged me.

'Alright treacle?' He kissed me on the neck and I wondered whether any of the tar on his lips had smudged over. Certainly it had.

'How's life, Gig?'

'Life's good, man. Come in, come in.' I came in. 'I thought you didn't see me.' His voice was sedate and cheerful, a slurred mix of the Geordie his parents gave him and the Midlands he'd never left.

'See you where?'

'In the car, outside yours, man – drove straight past me.'

'Ah, no. No—'

'Looked a bit stern – nearly clipped me on the way through.'

'If it's about the fifty…'

'No, no, don't be crazy man.' He slapped me lightly on the cheek, beckoned me into the living room and down onto the two-seater, which had been there as long as I'd been alive and still held the shape of his grandma and her cigar burns.

From under a cut-up copy of *Style* magazine on the coffee table he pulled out a huge bag of weed.

'I was round to show you this.' He put it to his nose. 'Pure Ukrainian Hulk. Off the ferry yesterday. Purest high on European soil, direct to my front door. What a world, you know?'

He plucked out a bud and started piecing it apart and into his grinder, Gloria.

'So what's with the bed-gown, man? You look flustered.'

Tightened the belt, leaned forwards.

'It's Sarah.' He looked at me, still rolling but suitably concerned. 'She's gone.'

'Again? I didn't know you'd been back together?'

'No…it's… No, we weren't. I went to get her back.'

'Nice.'

'But she wasn't there.'

'Ah.'

'She's gone.'

'Gone?'

'Yeah.'

'Where's she gone?' he asked.

'I don't know.'

'Shit.'

'She was staying at her sister's, but her sister doesn't know where she is.'

'You went round there?'

'I was going to talk to her.' Caught in the throat, too quick to suppress it.

'Course.' He stopped rolling, gesture so rare it fuelled the gloom.

When I closed my eyes I could see Sarah lying on our bed, rubbing a tattered piece of blue blanket between her thumb and her index finger, because at some point doing that had been a comfort. The day it disintegrated in the washing machine I lay at her feet for two hours to offer my hair as a surrogate. She said it wasn't the same.

I looked at the magazines on the coffee table. Keira Knightley. Laughed at the state I was in.

Gigger put down what he had of the spliff, reached across and put his hand on my thigh – his dad's hands, big and cracked, and yellow at the borders.

'I thought she'd come back when she'd had a bit of time.'

He shook his head softly, looked away from me, up at a spot on the wall.

'So did I,' he said.

I took a breath and Gigger took back his hand. There was a shuffle of pink slippers at the top of the stairs, but neither of us acknowledged that we heard it. I cleared my throat, took a while looking at the gargoyle faces sewn into the net curtains.

'I'm gonna find her,' I told him. 'Find her, get her back. Rattle the cage a bit, you know?'

'Rattle the cage, man – get out of the cage! Get her back, get yourselves to the seaside—'

'Paris.'

'Even better – get out of it all, man. Rock the boat.' He clicked his fingers and things brightened up. 'What do we know so far?'

'So far...' Breakdown receding. 'So far we know she's gone.'

'Disappeared – no note, no nothing man.'

'No note, no nothing. She'd been at her sister's house.'

He said 'Okay, what about phone?'

'I called her.'

'And?'

'Well she was fucking... It wasn't her.' I heard it again, this ghost of it. 'It was this laughing. Some cunt laughing.'

'A bloke?'

'Yeah, yeah. Our age, maybe a bit older.'

'What did he say?'

I looked at the gargoyles, bit the tip of my tongue.

'He said don't call here again.'

Gigger thought about that. His forehead scrunched together and his eyebrows twitched like a puzzled Scottie dog.

'Try it again, man. Speaker.'

I tried it again while he watched. This time it didn't ring at all.

'Hmm…' he said. 'Don't call here again?'

'And this proper fucking nasty laugh.'

'Like a harhar or more like a snigger?'

'Like a fucking…'

I gave it a go. Couldn't pull it off. He mulled it over.

'You know, it could always b—' A thud like a bellyflop echoed from the landing. He scowled with his eyes on the ceiling, then rolled them back down to me and picked up the spliff. 'Could always be a kidnapping.'

'A kidnapping?'

He was running his tongue along his teeth, nodding slowly.

'Precisely,' he said. 'I mean, I didn't think people still did kidnappings to be honest, but that's what Socks went down for – Sheila's son.'

'I thought it was murder?'

'Oh yeah, well he murdered them too, but it was originally just a kidnapping.'

'Jesus.'

'Got trigger happy when they didn't answer his calls by day two.'

'Day two?'

'Turned out he had one of the digits written down wrong.'

'Jesus Christ.'

'Yeah. Yeah…but I mean I'm not saying that's what's happened to your Mrs, man. I mean why'd someone want – I mean other than you – why'd someone want to… kidnap Sarah?' I hadn't considered it. 'Her family did have a fair bit in the bank, didn't they?'

'You think it could be that?'

'Mmm. Foolish.'

The thud came again, rattled the beads on the plastic chandelier.

Gigger licked along the gumline as he stood up and made his way over to the living-room door.

'These people and their trust in retail banking. Cash is king, McGann. Cash is king.' He pushed the door gently into the frame until it clicked.

'You think it could be the same guy?'

'Who could be the same guy?'

'The man with the hammer.'

'The hammer man.'

'You think it could be him?'

'What makes you think it is?'

'Don't you think it makes sense?'

'It's not making much – who in fuck's the hammer man?'

I caught him up.

He said 'I'd say there's a low chance. Can't say for sure.'

'What so that's a coincidence?'

'All I'm saying's I can't see how it helps a kidnapping to break into your place and try and bash your head in with a hammer.'

I thought about it.

'What if he came to negotiate?'

'I think don't get carried away with it man. You wanna find Sarah, you've gotta stay objective: we know she's been kidnapped, we don't wanna bias the investigation chasing red herrings. For all we know that fella was there to steal your copper pipes and you've frightened him into a rage coming out your bedroom while he's gan at it.'

He plucked a lock of nose hairs, sorted through them. The voice of reason.

'Stick to the facts,' he said. 'Rich family, isolated lass having a bad time. Treat her nice, take her in, handcuff her to a radiator and tell her parents pay the ransom and you'll kill her if they go to the police. Tale as old as time, man.'

'They'll kill her if we go to the police?'

'Well that's what I'd be telling them, wouldn't you?'

'Yeah…yeah.'

'On the other hand, there's a chance he was a henchman – there to take you out the picture and he's got greedy when he's seen the copper pipe. We're not counting anything out at this stage.'

I said 'You think there's more than one of them?'

He said 'Kidnappers rarely work alone, but again it depends what calibre of kidnapper we're dealing with here.' Knew if I could force an aneurism I could go back to bed. Gigger saw the veins, said 'I'd get after her with you if I didn't have the old bat.'

Breathed.

'It's my thing. I'll find her.'

He nodded.

'Can I give you a bit of cash, man? Help you along.'

'Petrol. I just need petrol… And a fizzy drink.'

Mrs Gigger had gone pneumatic now, but it was muffled by the door – distant enough to ignore. Gig flicked open his lighter and started on the spliff, which he'd finished rolling some time when I hadn't been looking at him. It crackled like they do in old films tobacco companies bankrolled.

He sat back and let the smoke float out of his mouth and his nose. Thick because the stuff was so fresh.

'Yeah, man.' he said. 'No problem.' Slowed his speech a few frames. 'Over in Marilyn.' He gestured to the photo-frame on the wall, with Marilyn Monroe in *The Seven Year Itch*, with the white dress – pink here – blowing up around her elbows. 'In-inside Marilyn.'

I went over to her, lifted the frame from its hook. The heels she had on looked slim enough to slot through the holes in the subway-grate. I took three twenties from behind her back and showed them to Gigger. He nodded and offered me the spliff. It was something you couldn't turn down.

The old lady repositioned herself above our heads and redoubled her drumming so the mounted handcuffs in the wall-cabinet joined in with the chandelier. Got a sense of the end of the world.

'I better put her stew on.' He stood up and took Gloria from the coffee table.

I looked at the clock on the wall and smoked and followed Gigger to the kitchen.

'Painted in here last week.' I scanned the walls. Slightly lighter shade of grey than before. 'Oil-based stuff – cover up the mould, you know. Need a step-ladder for the ceiling, though. Back's fucked,' he said.

Mould on the ceiling was oppressive. When you looked away, it closed in on the perimeter of brush strokes.

'Think I've got one. Could help you do it…after Paris.'

'Très bien mon ami.' On the chopping board he pulled from the drying-rack three collie dogs chased each other's tails. 'Told the agency about your bathroom yet?'

Potent. Seriously potent. I smoked some more and handed it over.

He asked me again.

'Oh, nah, they're still after me for the rent.'

'Fascists.' He chopped potatoes.

I asked him what day it was, but he said he couldn't be sure. Speculated that it felt like a Tuesday, which felt about right, but I needed confirmation.

He went to the medicine cabinet and took out his mom's tablet box.

'Either it's Tuesday, or the old lady's going to A&E again.' We listened for the stamping, which was much more spaced out now, but still there. 'Sounds fine.'

'Incredible stamina.'

'Fifteen years down the pits before she met dad,' he reasoned.

'I thought they didn't let women down the pits?'

'They didn't.'

Gigger worked at the leeks, pushed his hair back from his face over his ears. It was Tuesday. Tuesday Tuesday Tuesday. I looked around for a place to sit down and settled for leaning against the washing machine.

'Make enough for three days, man. Always enough for three days.'

'What were we talking about?'

'Mines, man. Fascists and mould.' He pushed in the ignition on the oven and held down the button, and I handed over the spliff again, unsure how I'd come to be holding it. He shook his head and lifted the pan onto another hob. 'Bit shy that one. Intermittent, you know? Need to take the whole thing apart one of these days.'

'Plan… The plan.'

'The plan, man.' Smoke ran out of his pores. 'Step one's a list of suspects.'

I said I couldn't think of anyone who'd even remotely

want to kidnap Sarah.

'And you're sure you haven't kidnapped her yourself?'

'Yeah.'

'Then I'm out of ideas too, man.'

Everything was already in a jar, and a dozen more jars were drying on the window sill.

He said 'So step one, part B: if there's nobody on the list, it's a brute-force attack.'

'Brute-force attack.'

'Get on the road, get looking for a breadcrumb – anything. You've been to her sister's, speak to her friends, get down her hairdresser's. Everywhere you can think of.'

'Everywhere I can think of.'

'Bloke on the checkout looks at her funny, postman sniffs her bank statement. Everywhere, everyone.'

I didn't say anything.

He said 'Actually fuck that, man. For a kick off I'd get down Rhoder & Dalt.'

'Rhoder & Dalt?'

'I've always said there's something suspicious about that place.' True of anywhere that wasn't here. 'Underhand, you know?'

'Start at Rhoder & Dalt.'

'Start at Rhoder & Dalt.'

He sipped a little broth, took a drag and held up the spliff. 'There's not a cat's chance in hell this has come off a boat from Ukraine. The shitbag Flatley's fleeced us for the last time, man.'

By the clock in the living room it was one-oh-nine.

He opened up Gloria and tapped the two sections against each other over the pan, stirred it in.

I said 'I better go, Gig.'

'Right-o,' he nodded, saw me to the front door. The

stamping upstairs tracked us through the house.

'Thanks,' I told him. He gave me a big Jeff Bridges smile and hit me in the arm.

'Call me in if you need back-up. I've got the katana under the bed from the set of *Kill Bill 2*.' He looked around for the neighbours and swayed on the balls of his feet on the doorstep. I checked my pocket for the sixty when I got in the car. 'McGann!' he said. 'Maybe put some underpants on first?'

4. The Photograph

I did. White t-shirt, black jeans, aftershave. Eyedrops. Didn't look good, but it didn't look so bad.

I filled the tank and drove into the city.

The lot brimmed full like always, but I lucked out and got a space on the ground floor, right by the entrance. Guy in a Fiesta hit the horn at me when I got out. He wasn't big. I gave him the treatment, told him to step out of the car, but he didn't like what he'd started anymore. There was an epidemic of entitled disabled people. Those toilets were for public use.

I worked at Rhoder & Dalt for seven years. It was an electrical logistics company – taking equipment to shops and banks and switching it on for them at twice what it cost. Like everyone, I started downstairs on the service desk, and then if you've got some white shirts and you can breathe with your mouth closed they trail Skittles up the stairs to the offices and lock the doors.

Somehow I was an Account Manager. Four of us in a dusty library of obsolete records from folded company accounts, pounding out emails to customers who hated us almost as much as we hated ourselves.

Sarah hated it too.

We got drafted in as seasonal staff and taken on a few months in because we showed up on time, and because the turnover on the service desk was so fast.

The old crowd on the floor bitched about Sarah because she didn't go out drinking with them. I told them I was a recovering addict, which by the third year was half true.

For both of us the job was a plug – something to keep us out of the hole until we got away somewhere better. We used to talk about what we'd do when that happened – dogs, cars, Paris. Eventually the plans we made got tied together, and then she'd link my arm when we were walking, and then she'd hold my hand.

There was a new guy at the front desk. He looked like he shaved his armpits with a wet razor and told people he followed The Bundesliga. Gave me a half-smile.

'I'm an old friend,' I said, although he hadn't asked.

'Mmm.' He popped the lid shut on his fineliner. 'An old friend of whom, if you don't mind?'

Whom?

'Oh everyone upstairs. Downstairs not so much, know what I mean?'

'Mmm.'

Guy Tuppence, said his badge. Tuppence had something in his teeth and he was working at it with a pink slug of a tongue while he looked me up and down. I tried to sparkle. It was some part of a leaf I thought, but I could only see it in flashes and every time it was shaped a little different.

'I used to manage some accounts here, see – HMV, the Post Office.'

'In which department?'

'Account Management.'

'Account Management?'

'Yeah, with Matt Hoffner, Lucas Sharp.'

'I don't know individual names, I'm afraid.' His hand went to the landline on his desk, started tapping through the directory. 'Whose line would you like me to call?'

'Actually, I was hoping I could surprise them. Just say hi.'

The hand hovered and then went up to his mouth to join the war.

I dropped him a wink. He looked thrown, like he thought he might have imagined it, but deep down he knew.

'Look, I was just passing by – if it's not a good time I can—'

He pulled whatever it was out and rolled it in his fingers. Could be Weetabix.

'No. You can go in, Mr...?'

'Gilbert.'

'Mr Gilbert.' He turned the guest book around for me. 'The time is twelve-forty-eight.' I looked puzzled and he joined the dots and gave me another 'Mmm' because smug tasted good. 'The clocks went back on Sunday, of course.'

'Of course.'

I took out a pen and signed the time and Gilbert Grape in my best set of loops.

'See Dortmund yesterday?'

'I'm sorry?' he said.

'Don't be.'

He gave me a guest pass-card and made a little note of

the number next to my name, and I scanned in and pushed through the barrier.

The place was under some huge new ownership, and they'd painted the hallway orange and thrown down red carpets, so it looked like the fire escape in a Wacky Warehouse. The glass doors that led out onto the floor were clouded so nobody knew there was an outside. I knelt down to see through the clear glass around the handle.

The Welshman, Jerry Matthews, was on his feet patrolling his sub-desk. Sarah had told me he wasn't taking a manager's wage and he'd probably step back down when Lydia Cole came back from leave. He was wearing the flabby navy suit he'd get buried in if they could find the casket to match.

I had to avoid Matthews, Jim Stant, and Carl Beatty – who I assumed was going to be wrapped around some intern teaching her about spreadsheets and halitosis, so when he opened the door into my head the best I could do was collapse gracefully and bounce back quickly.

'McGann!'

People swivelled on their chairs and took an ear out of their headsets. I took his hand.

'Mr Beatty, how are you?' Beatty was never in a good mood – supposedly he'd had to relocate to the Black Country from somewhere nice and Southern after he knocked somebody up on a night out in two-thousand and four. Now neither of them talked to him. The rest of us had never seen outside so he could fuck sympathy.

'What do you – Marc, what are you doing here?'

'Ah well that's great. That's just great,' I said, waving over his shoulder at a herd of people that squinted back at me, puzzled.

Beatty shared their sentiment.

I said 'Look, look, I'm just here to catch Sarah.' I gestured towards bay three, which had a newly orange pillar in the way of it. 'Shall I…'

He still looked confused. I rounded him in the doorway and negotiated through the maze of tables in the direction of Sarah's desk.

Up behind the glass at the top of the stairs you could see Stant's office and the boardroom, but the blinds were closed and the lights were off in both.

Stant had started just after us. Every Christmas party for five years I gave him the Mr Rim Job Trophy for sucking management's tract, and on the sixth year he didn't show up.

When the top job came up Sarah pushed me to apply, filled the forms out in my name. I managed the biggest accounts, knew the role, didn't worry people when I smiled at them. But Jimmy had bought Mick Tompkins an extra-creamy cappuccino every morning for three years. It was a no-brainer. Mick stepped down and told me he thought I'd think his recommendation was fair – he'd chosen the hardest working man on the staff. It was going to be a difficult few years for the company, and that was what they needed.

When Stant got the job and the takeover talk and the efficiency savings started, he looked straight at the Account Managers because there were four of us on the big twenty-five k. The other three had kids. I said I'd go. Never told Sarah that was why.

I made it around the pillar.

'Marc, Sarah's left Rhoder & Dalt,' Beatty said from

closer behind me than I'd thought he'd be.

'When?'

'When? Over a fortnight ago, now.'

'So where did she go?'

'I don't know where she went.'

On her desk there was a slim guy with brown-blonde hair in a purple jumper, and I couldn't help thinking how much he looked like me. His face was younger, though, and his hair was gummed into a sharp flick at the front.

I went to the metal drawers next to his legs and he wheeled away to give me space, watching me, locked into the service script – a set of flow charts that all ended in relinquishment of responsibility on Rhoder & Dalt's part. Beatty marked me tight. Tuppence was in the room now, and he was speaking into a walkie-talkie, looking guilty. Necks stretched up over dividers to get a good look at what was going on. The blinds upstairs didn't move.

The top drawer was stiff but I knew Sarah always left it unlocked because she had trouble holding onto a set of keys, so I yanked at it until it came towards me. It was empty except for a stapler with SS tippexed onto the face – Sarah's initials – and a box of chamomile tea. I looked up at Beatty. Beatty looked down at me and then back towards Tuppence, who was standing next to a six-four meathead, dressed all in black. I didn't see myself winning that one but in the interest of rattling cages I sort of fancied finding out.

The second drawer came out more easily. I pushed around a mess of aspirin wrappers and chapsticks, and various book-tagging sticky notes Sarah had bought at an outlet stationary store one Sunday two years ago.

Upstairs a window hinged open. Behind it there was the tall shape of a man, standing back, looking through at me. The light against the glass obscured his face, and then a pair of black trousers stepped between us.

'Sir, I'm going to have to escort you from the premises,' said the meathead. His chest hung over me like a cliff-face. On the top of it, hairless and annoyed about it, was the red face of a sex-starved bull. Beatty was rubbing his hands together, squirming and nodding around at the watching faces. I closed the second drawer and pulled at the bottom one, but it jammed. 'Sir, I don't want to have to be physical,' he said, although the way his hands were clenched made it unconvincing.

Felt this rolling desperation. Knew if I didn't find whatever I was looking for here I was going to have to waterboard a hairdresser who didn't know what I was talking about. Without something to follow, I was just drifting, and I didn't have time to be drifting. I jerked at the drawer with both hands, braced against the other two with my foot.

'Sir.' He put his hand on my shoulder. I jerked again, and it cracked and reeled out towards me. 'Sir!' he growled at me, clamped his hands around my forearm. The drawer was deeper than the previous two, but that only made it look even more empty. I ran my free hand around the inside edges, and the meathead strained to pull me onto my feet. Nothing. My doppelgänger was finishing up his call now, and he was frowning at me like he'd just noticed the similarities.

'Mr McGann,' Beatty pleaded, a bead of sweat hanging like in a cartoon to the tip of his nose.

'Sir!' The meathead came again, almost ripped my shoulder out of its socket tugging me into him.

'Hey. Hey! Hey! No problem, okay? No problem,' I said, 'I'm coming.'

I wriggled my arm free and tried to look easy. Perfect score of doors slammed on me wasn't looking good. No-one here cared that Sarah had gone. The world had carried on as if she'd never been there at all.

The meathead put his hand on my back and nudged me towards the doors. I looked at the window upstairs, but there was no-one behind it. Tuppence was listening to the walkie-talkie and whispering sheepishly back at it. Eventually he crept away.

I wanted to scream out her name. How could it be business as usual? Where was the concern? I looked around at them, spinning, repeating themselves. Castrated. Lobotomised.

Beatty had wiped the sweat away and was working up a new batch. He opened up his body and gestured at the doors, and I couldn't think of a reason not to leave.

Jerry Matthews, who had been watching from a distance, came away from his team and opened one of the doors for me, and Beatty peeled off back to his intern.

'Sorry about this, Marc. You know wha' Jim's like about the accounts.'

I stopped, and again the stubby fingers jabbed into me.

'Where is she, Jerry?'

He looked sad. He always looked sad really.

'She just stopped turnin' up, Marc,' he said. 'An extended break, I thought.' Then he slowed away from our pace. 'To recover, you know?' I got jabbed through the barrier and Jerry disappeared behind the fog.

I wondered about that.

Then someone called my name and we stopped.

Tuppence, who had somehow beaten us back to the front desk, came around holding something.

'Mr...McGann,' he said. And he turned his head and

looked at me with this reloaded smugness. 'This was left in your old pigeonhole.'

Brown unstamped envelope.

I snatched it away and he dug his nails in, scored tramlines across my capitalised name.

Felt like thin card inside.

'When?' I said.

'Sir,' the meathead said, holding the door for me to leave. Tuppence smirked and walked backwards towards the desk.

'Get his pass-card please, Olly.'

He did, and then he shut me out.

I hadn't eaten since breakfast and I wasn't sure I'd eaten that.

I went to Patterson and Son – greasy spoon just around the corner from work which made it policy to undercut the company canteen.

Sat up at the counter on a wooden stool that had one leg shorter than the others, and Patterson Sr. wiped a ring of tea from in front of me and took my order. I dried the patch off with the clean part of a dirty napkin, put the envelope there and looked it over.

One of the two men asked me if I wanted pickle. I didn't.

Brown envelope, blue ink. Full name. No address.

Toyed with the idea of patiently trying to work out if that combination meant anything. Then tore into it, pulled out the photo.

Half a photo. Half a polaroid photo of me. Ripped down my right arm, which was burned, flopped out of a white and navy towel I'd never owned, all of it obscuring any distinguishing details of the shingle beach behind me.

Above the towel my face was red too – letterbox red – looking off into the rip with the same baffled expression the sneeze guard was reflecting at me now.

Searched around for the other half, turned out the envelope. No.

Patterson Jr. took a steak-knife from the rack and started sawing at a kilo of cheddar from the Tetris wall of them in the fridge. Asked me again if I was having pickle. Told him I wasn't.

The place was empty apart from me and the Pattersons. A redhead wearing a green business suit opened the door, then came to her senses and left. Patterson Sr. didn't look up. He was standing by the fryer, doubled over a book of crossword puzzles with no pen.

Patterson Jr. pressed the palm of his hand into the top of my sandwich, plated it up and cut it into triangles. He carried it over to me, clattered it down.

'One for sorrow,' he said.

'What?'

'It's on the back of that you twat.'

I turned the thing around and Jr. slipped into the gents.

He was right: dug into the back of the half-photo with the same blue pen as the envelope: One for sorrow. I read it out loud and the old man glanced over.

'Two for joy,' he said, switched back to the crossword.

One for sorrow.

I turned it back over, looked at myself in the towel.

One for sorrow.

Towel I'd never owned.

We'd been away with Lucy and her husband only once, when an ash-cloud from a volcano in Madeira stranded them in the UK. Sarah suggested the four of us go to the summerhouse that their parents had left when they'd gone to Switzerland.

It rained for six days in a row. The three of them sat watching Tim Robbins videos on the living-room TV. I spent most of the time in the bedroom in the garage, playing a copy of *The Wrath of Cortex* on their dad's old PS2 with no memory card. I had to play it all the way through from the beginning every time somebody turned it off. Lucy did twice, explained to me how watching films I didn't want to was part of being an adult.

On the day we went to leave the sun came out. Lucy insisted that we go to the beach before we set off. She wouldn't swim herself, because she hadn't been able to find a suitable bathing-suit for the English sea, but me and Sarah just had to.

I lied that we'd forgotten our towels, so Lucy gave us hers.

My stomach contracted. I saw the fridge at the summerhouse, covered top to bottom in blurred polaroids and tacky magnets.

And then I knew where she was.

5. The Trip

Shots of rain bounced off the bonnet and the road. Couldn't see the car in front until they hit the brakes.

We'd hit a storm half-way down the M5, and the wind buffeted through the new side panel.

I hogged the fast lane.

Sticky. It was sticky and kind of freezing at the same time, and I was shirtless because I thought that might do something for it. Sometimes I leaned forwards and peeled my back off the white leather.

I opened a beer from the footwell with my teeth.

The sat-nav was fifteen years old and it didn't like cities or storms. I threw it in the glovebox next to the knife, put on Drivetime. Maybe two hours from Tolten – the resort where the Salt family stored the things they didn't want cluttering the Swiss mansion.

There was a dream I couldn't put to bed, where I'm riding shotgun in my own car on some summer day. We hit a downslope that looks like *Bullitt* in San Francisco, and

I look over and no-one's got the wheel. I scramble to get across but it's all too quick and I get pinned back against the seat. It's like I'm glued down, and I'm reaching for the brake with my right leg but it doesn't stretch far enough. After that I don't know what happens. I guess that's all.

The more I drank, smoked, the easier I got to sleep, but the worse the dreams got, and the less I liked to sleep at night.

Being alone in the dark was terrible.

The beer went flat fast, and it wasn't doing the trick for the dry-mouth Gigger's weed had given me, so I pulled into the services at Sethendon and slid across and out. The umbrella Sarah bought me was on the hook at the flat like always. I took my t-shirt and held it over my head through the car-park, put it on when I got inside.

'Can I take two minutes of your time, sir?' asked a kid in a charity lanyard outside the men's room.

I took a leak.

Smith's was overbright, stocked full of shiny wank. They taxed drivers five quid for a sandwich in a cardboard box, crisps, and Irn Bru, made you call it a deal.

I took the Irn Bru alone, climbed under the theme park queue barriers to the till.

'Hello?' I called around.

A dumpy girl in the blue polo and black trousers was teasing herself fronting up the Hobnobs. She held a finger up at me.

'Hi, sorry...'

'Just a moment, sir.' Two fingers now.

I waited. Looked through the scratchcards and wondered if that e-liquid stuff tasted as good as it looked. She moved onto crisps.

'Excuse me – sorry, I just have…'

'I'll be with you in a moment, sir.'

Waited again. Wished you could buy individual chewing gum, like a pick 'n' mix. Unscrewed the cap and took a drink. That's when she got interested. Mumbled something in Scottish and sighed and waddled over.

I tried handing her a pound. She didn't look at it, just looked through my face like I was the reason for it all, scanned the bottle in my hand.

'That's one twenty-nine, sir.'

I looked down at my pound.

'What?'

'That will cost you one pound and twenty-nine, sir.'

Clearly fucking with me.

'One twenty-nine?'

'One twenty-nine, sir.'

'It says ninety-nine p.'

I held the bottle up to show her. She didn't look down.

'That's a recommended retail price, sir. We reserve the right to charge what it is we please.'

We? My wallet was in the car, but I patted my trousers for it anyway.

'Look, I've only got five…six, seven, nine p.'

I dropped it in her hand and she smiled like I'd given her the clap.

'The price is one twenty-nine.'

Now she was speaking a little louder. A family in matching yellow raincoats had come in and were browsing the magazines while dad took some sneaky ones at the top shelf. The little boy didn't like the look of me, and in the CCTV screen above Dumpy's head neither did I.

'Look, I'll just have a water then. Leave that one.'

'No, sir,' she said.

'...'

'This bottle has been opened, sir. It must be purchased.'

I tried to hush it down. 'I'm in a hurry, alright? What option have I got?'

'Sir, you must pay the full amount.'

'Look...my girlfriend's been kidnapped.'

'Do not threaten me, sir, or I will have to inform security.' She turned it up a notch more. Ann Summers 2009 over again.

'I'm not threatening you. I'm explaining the situation.'

'Is everything alright?' said the raincoat man, holding a copy of *Total Film* over his crotch.

'It's fine.'

'I was asking the lady. Is everything alright?'

'I said it's fucking fine.'

'There's no need to swear, sir.'

'There really is no need to swear.'

Cunt.

'I'm not being threatening – I just want a drink. Have you got twenty p?'

'Sir, I'm going to have to ask you to leave.'

'What?'

'Please leave the store, sir.'

'You've got my drink and my fucking pound.'

Raincoat took a step closer. The other two backed off.

'There is no need to swear. There are children present,' he said.

'I'll swear if I want to fucking swear.'

Everyone put on their appalled expressions, and I got tired of being the twat their pathetic little psychodrama.

'Look.' I snatched the bottle out of her hand and made a mess of hurdling the barriers. Raincoat flinched away in case I was coming for him, and boy would I have liked to, but now wasn't the time. Now was the time for mature decisions. Now was the time for running.

'Sir! Sir! Security!'

The security guard was playing slots in the arcade when I flew past him, pretending he couldn't hear the commotion cos he just span three raspberries.

He was out looking for me by the time I made it to Syn. I tailed a Toyota Avensis through the petrol station forecourt, chin on the dash.

Fuck the Scottish.

Floored it as far as Bristol, where we clogged against an overturned campervan. According to the radio the ambulances couldn't get through a flood on the junction. Some heroes parked in a shield around the wreck, blocked any chance of a path through the debris. A few got out to try and help. By the looks on their faces, it didn't matter when the ambulance got there.

I took out the photo, held it on the steering wheel.

I'd never groomed well. Didn't get along with my barber, couldn't get the hang of a razor. Around me the towel looked oversized and my shoulders poked through like prison spikes on playground fences. People said I looked like Rik Mayall. I didn't like the sound of that.

Sarah looked too good for Rik Mayall, and people in Oldon got a real kick out of reminding you about it. When I paid the rent, bought the food and the things she liked from the jewellery show she was hooked on, I didn't care what they said. When we lost the house and sold it all, then it started to get to me.

They scooped up the mess and things opened up. The water cleared and the clouds thinned out and for five minutes we all took it easy thinking how we could be next. Then we forgot about it.

I was clipping eighty-five. We all were. I saw the lights go up on a black BM and everyone eased off but I knew it was me. He moved in behind and I rode him for as long as it took me to work out a story.

Six-two and prettier in his own mirror than mine, he straightened up his shirt and strolled on over. For most of the time we were talking he seemed to be smoothing his hair in the reflection on the window, but every time I tried to catch him he was back on me.

He asked me if I knew how fast I was going.

'I think maybe seventy-five.'

He told me it was faster than that, and I was swerving a little.

'Swerving?'

A little, he'd have let it pass if not for the speed. Where was I going?

'I'm going on holiday. On a holiday.'

He looked at the back seats for a suitcase or a body.

'You're going on a—'

'A holiday of sorts, I mean.'

'A holiday of sorts?'

'Yes.'

He shook his head.

'Sir, I'm going to have to write you a ticket.'

'I'm going to have a dog destroyed.'

'You're going to have a...'

'My cocker spaniel. Lucy.'

'Your cocker spaniel?'

'Lucy, yes, I'm going to have her euthanised.'

He looked at the back seat again, which was covered in a brown throw and a dozen empty Monster Munch packets. No dog.

'Where's the dog?'

'She's going by train. Doesn't like the motorways.'

'Sir, I'm going to have to write you a ticket—'

'I've had an emotional day. That bitch was my life.' I felt around for something sharp. Considered the glove box. 'Surely there's another way we can work this out,' I said.

He started to ask me if I was trying to bribe him, but then his radio crackled some numbers and he told me to hold on.

'Reddinger, two-five-six-eight. What was that?'

The man on the other end was distant. He said 'Urgent incident at Sethendon service station. Possibly intoxicated suspect driving an orange BMW 330, southbound.'

He squinted into the car. I looked relaxed, drank my Irn Bru, palmed a spare door key from inside the Urban Hymns cassette.

'Orange Three-Series?'

'Affirmative.'

He looked into the car, down his nose at me, then he shook his head.

'On my way.'

'Officer, I'll slow down.'

'Sir, is that a beer bottle down there?'

'No. That? No, that's flat. You can try it.' I offered it up to him.

'Slow down. Calm down. The roads are wet and there are some volatile people on them.'

'God bless you.' I started her up, leaned out of the window and blew a kiss at the back of his head, stalled a couple of times while I got my eye back in.

Gigger said everybody wants a piece of you: the law, work, landlords. They want you locked away, feeding them. Said we needed to get out of the cage and he was right. Sarah had the key to mine, I had a hammer for hers.

6. The Summerhouse

I parked a dozen houses down, walked up the hill.

The place was a stack of extensions, bursting like tumours out of what had probably been a pretty nice cottage. It was made out of a lot of glass that looked like it hadn't been cleaned since last time I saw it. The curtains were shut tight.

Mrs Dixon, next door, was getting the cat's bowls from the step, holding a roll of paper towels thicker than her waist. I dipped down behind the front hedge. She was humming something like 'Mr Bojangles'.

Dixon – Joan – had to be in her eighties now, one of a small group who lived on the road the whole year round. She was close with the Salt family, though not really Sarah. I wondered if she'd know what happened between us. Either way, deaf in one ear, so incapable of quiet conversation, she had to be avoided if I didn't want everybody on the south coast knowing I was there.

From inside the summerhouse came something like a plate smashing. I ducked down, tried to see through the gaps in the leaves, took a quick shower in the rain they'd been saving. The kitchen blind swayed slightly against the pane, then back into place, and it felt like the lights dimmed around me.

Down below the gardens, around Dixon's house, was an alley that led to the back gate. I went quietly. Took the steps down to it and undid the padlock, open for the landscape gardener, who'd either retired, died, or taken an abstract turn involving knee-high grass and headless gnomes.

The fifteen or so wooden stairs up to the decking had been seized by a slippery looking legion of algae. At the top of them were a set of sliding doors at the back of the kitchen, a stained-glass cartwheel window that led onto the hallway, and finally, in a single-glazed chequered frost, a bathroom window that didn't lock properly because I'd snapped the latch off five years before. That was the way in.

Taking the stairs was going to leave me exposed, and the bannister was notoriously weak. Really the whole place needed a revamp. I thought about climbing the drainpipe. I'd climbed drainpipes before, but this one looked like it might not be made for climbing. It was plastic, and the bolts looked loose, and at the top of it a malnourished seagull stood waiting like a nervous alarm system.

I thought about the voice on Sarah's phone. Built a picture around it – half Hammer Man, half gorilla or some kind of bear or something.

Wondered again if I knew him. If she knew him. And it boiled my stomach the idea he'd got around me, and it boiled my stomach that I'd buried myself away, left her exposed.

Maybe that was what One for Sorrow meant. If not then I didn't have a clue, and that made me feel even worse because I knew I was supposed to. I knew Sarah trusted me to.

The throw over the back seat of the car was more or less the same dirty brown as the stairs and the decking. I jogged back, burned a little anxiety, dragged it out and brushed it off. More a rug than a throw – had some real thickness. When I put it over my head it funnelled straight up and stayed there instead of cloaking me, so I looked like the back half of a pantomime horse.

Camouflage was alright outside. When I was through the bathroom window there'd be nowhere to hide. I opened the glove box and took out the knife. Kept it folded away in the leather sheath, in the back pocket of my jeans.

Made it back. Except for the knife and the horse suit things were the same. That was reassuring. I pushed the gate closed, flattened out on my belly and dragged myself up the stairs like a slug.

Two from the top I gave my elbows a break, folded back a few inches, stole a look at the windows. And in the bathroom I saw a face.

Pixelated by the chequered window: green eyes, shag of black hair and then gone.

No sound. Nothing louder than the blood in my ears.

I recoiled into the rug and stayed there, waited for the vacuum sound of the doors sliding open. Waited for the man, the men – the kidnappers – to come for me. Waited to pounce. I'd take one's legs away from him, slice a calf open, throw him into the bannister – test it out. Then for the second – if there was a second – burst out of the rug, swing for the groin to get him moving, then dive for the neck.

I gripped the knife.

Silence.

My trainers dug in hard against the algae stairs. Held position. Wondered if already he was standing above, ready to crack me. Lifted my head. Still nothing. Still the doors stood watch. Either he hadn't seen me at all or now he was waiting, hidden. Whichever it was, I had to move fast.

I hauled over the last two steps and stayed on the deck. Waited. Checked the bathroom window. And then in this sweet manoeuvre I span out of the horse, left it flat on the wood, and pinned myself against the summerhouse wall between the cartwheel and the kitchen.

The seagull-alarm had seen enough. It dropped down over the bedroom-garage at the bottom of the garden and off to meet the clouds that were closing in on the bay.

I was fifty feet high, on stage, and in front of me a hundred allotment gardens roared me on and the same buzz from the hammer fight rushed through me.

I was tough, limber. Had a knife.

Boiling veg from Dixon's kitchen sent plumes of steam over the fence and they hung around like dry ice.

The music played me in.

Three.

I blew snot out of a nostril and it hit the deck, wondered how much blood you should worry about.

Two.

Slid over to the bathroom, visualised it: in, doors off the hinges, slash his neck, blood everywhere, save Sarah.

One.

'What are you gonna do with the money Mr McGann?'

'We're gonna go to Paris, Bruce!'

Grabbed the window, threw it open, got a foot through a spectrum of empty shower gel bottles somehow without knocking one off. Hoisted up. Perched. Tested the sink, which cracked away from the wall when I gave it any weight.

Landing strip looked ropey – no bath mat, just tile, with what looked like a muddy print from the kind of boot the Hammer Man had on.

Dixon was humming again on the other side of the fence, getting the washing in. Sounded like a nursery rhyme I couldn't find the words to.

'Mr McGann, you have ninety seconds remaining!'

Pulled off my trainers and socks, threw them backwards into the crowd, sat between the shower gels, and with the hype of everyone spurring me on I got in my head I could lift my body just with my arms and propel myself over the footprint and out through the door.

'Stop the clock.'

I peeled the shower curtain off of me, pulled my top half out of the bath and checked I still had my ankles and the knife. Hard to say exactly what had happened. On the top of my head there was already a golf ball that was only going to get bigger. I hadn't heard the sound I'd made, but there wasn't much hope nobody else had.

Smeared across the tiles and my feet and the back of my leg, the muddy footprint smelled unmistakably like shit.

I switched on the shower for a second, tried washing some of it off in case Sarah thought I'd done it myself.

'Start the clock – eighty seconds.'

The hallway was dark, and it smelled like the back of a kebab house. Or I did. I stepped carefully, took the knife out and held it low, ready to jab.
Kicked open door one –

'You've won a beautiful washer and dryer set, generously donated by our friends at Hotpoint, for all your shit and blood stain washing needs!'

Swept the laundry room, went back to the hallway.
Kicked open door two—

'You're the proud owner of a second hand single mattress, complete with a lovely velvet floral sheet. Sixty seconds left!'

Back to the hallway.
There was an inch of light coming through from the kitchen – door three. I held my breath and watched it. Stroked the lump on my head. Hell of a hit. Then I kicked it wide.
'Ha!'
Pirouetted through the half-light, half tripped over a laundry basket in the middle of the floor.

'Fifty seconds!'

On the sides and on the floor there were scraps of food and spilled milk mixed up with a few shards of the smashed plate I'd heard when I arrived. The table was clean except for a copy of a newspaper.

I ran to the bedrooms, kicked open doors, pulled open curtains. Empty.

In Sarah's and Lucy's and the master bedrooms the beds were untouched. No Sarah. Nobody. Not anymore.

'Sarah?' I called out in desperation more than anything else.

'Thirty seconds Mr McGann. If you don't find her, you lose everything you've won so far!'

Took the stairs back down. Lump throbbed. Had they heard me come in? Made it out the front in time? I kept the knife ready.

'Sarah?'

The newspaper on the table was the *Financial Times*. Dated a week ago. I picked it up, read the headline, and behind it on the fridge, in the mess of Lucy's horrific selfies and King Arthur magnets, I saw her. Took the half-polaroid out of my pocket, stepped to the fridge, and slotted the two pieces together. Me and Sarah on Tolten Bay, her bent double, laughing at the burned mess of my face, and the ringlets the salt water left in her hair skipped like schoolgirls around a maypole.

I'd never really realised what a great picture it was. 'There are no photos of us, Marco. Everyone else takes photos!' I didn't like them. Always too awkward, stiff. But—

'Twenty seconds!'

I shook it off.

If she'd been handcuffed to a radiator like Gigger said I couldn't see how she'd reached the fridge, or a blue pen to write on it, or an envelope, or a letterbox, but Sarah was resourceful – she'd found a way to get it to me, knew I'd come.

Maybe I'd come too late. I didn't want to think about it.

'Ten!'

Dropped the paper, kept the polaroid, slid open the back doors.

'Nine!'

And below where the clouds had swallowed the sea view, across the headless meadow, there was an open window – the skylight in the garage.

'Eight!'

I ran, taking the steps three, four at a time so the crawling up felt really absurd.

'Seven!'

Across the lawn there were my shoes and socks and little mines of cat shit.

'Six!'

At the glass door I could see a bulb hanging down. Took a few seconds to gather myself—

'Five! Four! Three! Two!'

Then cracked down the handle and burst into the room.

On the bed in front of me there were bloody sheets balled up. There were bottles of wine and food packaging. Then I felt a terrific hot pain in the back of my head. And then another one. The second was overkill.

7. The Garage

I had the taste of blood where presumably I'd bitten my tongue on the way to the ground.

Rain spat at my face through the skylight.

I was sitting on a wooden chair with blue rope tying my hands behind my back and my ankles together. Above my head the naked bulb that half lit the room swayed in the breeze.

I was alone and incapacitated. Neutered. They had my knife, my shoes, my girlfriend. I didn't know what they had planned for me. In terms of assets I was worthless, but what I knew made me important, dangerous even.

Outside it was starting to get dark.

I knew they wouldn't be far away – they weren't going to risk leaving me to spill the beans when I figured a way out. I swung right and left, and the chair screeched against the floor, moved a couple of inches towards the cabinet with the TV on it. The PlayStation was out. Someone had been playing *Spyro: Dawn of the Dragon*. Not a good game. I hauled forwards again, harder this time, strained to hear anybody coming, then again harder still. When I was close enough to reach for the drawer with my mouth I did. Probably I could have used my lips but instead I got my teeth around the metal knocker-like thing and eased it out. The wires drawer – wires, extensions, batteries, controllers. Also a pair of nail scissors for cutting ties. Leaned in again with my teeth, plucked them out. I bobbed twenty apples in a minute at the Black Country Millennium All Schools Summer Fair – came second to a boy using orthodontic headgear like a lobster cage and held his head under until he handed over the chocolate. Anyway so I plucked out the scissors, and the only way I was gonna get them into my hands was either some miraculous flick and catch, or by being on the floor. The flick was disappointing. I watched them spin in slow motion past my left eye and hit me in the forehead, then flop down beneath my feet. So I wanted to fall in a way that didn't aggravate the injuries I'd already got. I rocked forwards and balanced myself on my feet and two legs of the chair, then eased myself sideways and let my weight and the chair fall against the cabinet. I was inching downwards when the door opened and a black cat with green eyes ran in with a jingly bell.

''Scuse me,' she said.

'Mrs Dixon!' I'd hit the floor facing away from the door so I couldn't see her, but I knew the voice. 'Jesus. Jesus Mrs Dixon, quickly.'

'Oh my God, oh my God,' she was saying, and she ran around to the front of me so I could see her sandals and her pruney feet. I looked up. In her hand she was holding an empty pressure cooker. 'Oh my God.'

'Mrs Dixon I've been kidnapped.'

'Kidnapped? Oh my God.'

'It's okay. I'm okay. The scissors. Get the scissors, cut the rope.'

She bent down to me, and I saw that around the handle of the pan there was a roll of duct-tape, and I stopped talking.

She had her hand over her mouth.

The cat was stroking itself against my back, purring.

8. The Snoop

She put me in her husband's armchair, showed me how to recline it and set it to vibrate. I did both. The cat kept circling to get on my lap but I wasn't having it. Everything was pink and flowery, except the urn on the mantelpiece that was white and blue and looked like a cookie jar. She was playing Al Jolson from a pretty old PC on a state of the art speaker set-up.

I asked why she had the duct tape.

She pressed her fingers to her head and shook it.

She said 'It's just what you see them do isn't it? Get the mouth shut.'

'Get the mouth shut?'

'So they can't scream.'

She tapped at her temple nervously, said 'You had a knife, and you were running in the garden with no socks on. It all happened at once, and then you were on the floor and I thought if he gets up he's not going to take kindly to you, Joan.'

I fancied giving her a whack, even things up.

She said 'What were you doing, running around like that, my love?'

None of your fucking business, my love.

'Chopping.'

Bored of my own lies already – tell the old cunt to get her nose out, have a bit of money off her and get back on the trail while things were hot.

'Chopping a bit of veg.' Jabbed towards her a couple of times. 'Roast dinner. Went to see if there was a gravy jug in the garage.'

On the table next to her chair my brown rug was folded neatly, with my trainers and my socks on top of it and the knife over to one side.

She shook her head again, went to the freezer and got me a fresh bag of petit pois for my lumps, swapped them for the sweetcorn. When she looked at the bruises she whistled through her throat like a punctured dinghy.

I told her forget about it because she was getting on my nerves apologising.

'Now,' she said, 'I always get these two mixed up. So your wife's name's Lucy, isn't it?'

'For my sins.'

'And your sister-in-law is the younger girl with the curly hair – Sarah – that's right isn't it?'

Quick bash round her head with the pressure cooker, square things up. Conversation over.

'That's right.'

'So,' she reached across and patted her hand on my leg. 'I am sorry dear, but what was your name?'

'Erm. Ian. Ian Salt.'

The cat had given up getting onto me now. It was standing by the table with my things on, looking at the knife and back to me.

'Oh, so you took your wife's name?'

'No.' Was she trying to trip me up? 'No, my name was already Salt.'

'Oh, well that's convenient love.'

I was trying to de-recline the chair, but the vibrations and the concussion and maybe low blood sugar were triggering this mild euphoria I didn't want to interrupt.

She asked if the two of us were down here for a holiday. I said it was actually some pretty sombre business involving a cocker spaniel with terminal stomach cancer. Told her I didn't want to get into it.

Looked at me with this desperation, like she hadn't entertained in years. Maybe she could work on her welcoming tactics.

The cat had crawled to the top of the chair behind her, competing for attention. It was doing that thing where they knead the fabric, staring at me intensely.

She said 'I didn't know if you wanted me to wash your trousers, love…' Glanced down accusingly at the still wet streak of shit that ran up my right calf.

'I slipped. In the bathroom. It was on the floor…I mean it was already on the floor when I got there. Just this puddle of it.'

'Oh!' Without warning she flew over at the cat and startled out of its kneading into a blind panic and off up the stairs. 'Kovac! You dirty little so and so!' she shouted after it. 'I'm so sorry. He's been at the dairy again. It's been everywhere. Oh my God.'

'Don't worry about it—'

'I wondered if Sarah had been giving him milk or ice cream.'

I turned the vibration off, sat up.

'Sarah?'

'Yes, because I know she'd been having him in the house, and I mean I don't mind if he gets fed—'

'You've seen Sarah?'

'Well...yes dear.'

I put my hand in my pocket. Pinched together the two pieces of picture.

'They were staying down in the garage, you see.'

I felt the grief, like someone pulling a piece of string out of your chest.

'For how long?'

She thought about it, moonwalked back to where the stairs met the living room and picked up a purple diary from the phone table. She opened to where the ribbon was, licked her fingers and swiped back a few pages.

'Six days. Up until yesterday morning, love.' She looked up above her glasses at me and I tried to be cool.

On the day Sarah left me I offered to drive her to her sister's house, but she took the bus instead. She seemed relaxed. Drugged, like a morning commute. She sat on the back row, and I waved to her when the doors closed, but she didn't see.

The roses in the wallpaper unravelled and wilted, twisted into knots and strangled the life out of each other.

'I'm putting you some chips on dear, and I don't want any arguments, okay?'

I stood up and followed Dixon to the kitchen, fought back a throat full of sick.

'Who was she with?'

She closed the oven door with her heel.

'Oh, well I assumed it was the new man, you know. Had his arm around her.'

New man? She didn't know what she was talking about. I was gonna get his eyes out and drag him around by them. Cut his hands off, staple his lips together, rent a garage somewhere to keep him in. What fucking new man?

I tried to smile. She was bent over, looking in the bottom drawer of the freezer like she'd lost something. If I could see the top of her underwear over her skirt then she was wearing a thong, so I assumed I was seeing something else.

Fucking new man.

'I suppose it's one I haven't met. What did he look like?' I said.

She came back up again looking puzzled, adjusted her glasses.

'What did he look like? I'd say not dissimilar to you, dear. White fella. Slightly darker hair, an inch or two taller.' She leaned her head on the side now, and she said 'More groomed maybe, but I'd say he didn't have your looks.'

She went back to the freezer, rifled through all of the drawers this time.

'Did she look happy?'

'Happy?'

Did she ever look happy?

'When they got here they were having a bit of a spat. I don't like to snoop, you know, so I only had half an eye on it, and it's not safe for a seventy-two year old to stand on the stairs for too long but that window up there was the only place where I could get a clear view, you see.'

She had her hands on her hips, half her mind on the peas I had behind my head.

What kind of a retard can't tell a new man from a kidnapper?

'They were shouting and cursing a bit, you know—'

Oh were they.

'I'd say nothing serious. Just tired and peckish after the trip like yourself. Lovely car – one of the new sporty Jaguars.'

If I responded to that I don't know what I said.

Dixon said 'I didn't see much of them after that, you know – kept to themselves, didn't pop over. But Sarah never tended to.'

She handed me a china cup of watery coffee I hadn't seen her boil.

'Neither of you have got any kiddies yet, have you?'

'Your peas,' I said, handed her the bag. She muttered some lecture at herself about forgetfulness and filled a pan while I slipped over to the pantry – all booze, no food – added a nip of whiskey to the coffee.

The cat had regained its nerve, joined us in the kitchen.

'You look tired yourself, love. Terrible about your poor spaniel. Must be awful.'

I was tired. Really exhausted, and I couldn't make any sense of what Dixon was saying because of the head trauma and everything was draining. Poured a little more whiskey.

The other half of a polaroid photo and a week old copy of the *Financial Times* didn't exactly make a treasure map. I just wanted somebody to tell me what to do, where to go, and I'd do it.

I said 'You didn't speak to either of them at all after they arrived? They didn't say where they were going?'

She set a timer for the chips, but her eyes stayed on me, patted me down.

She knew then I wasn't who I said I was. I straightened my face, counted heartbeats, tried everything I could not to look like the Wolf.

And maybe from a pocket I couldn't see, or maybe from somewhere she'd hidden it away, the old lady again pulled out the purple diary. Again turned past the silver ribbon, this time a single page, to yesterday.

'I did…' She thought about it some more. 'I did overhear something.'

The Lord is my shepherd.

'I only write it down because my memory's not what it was, and…' Fiddled with the chain on her glasses. 'I was in the greenhouse, you see love. Giving it a spruce – which I really shouldn't be doing myself, but my Jack used to do it and I don't like to let it get too far out of hand or he'd be turning in his grave, you know.'

I wondered who she had in the cookie jar.

'As I said, I didn't see Sarah again. She was locked away. But when I was down in the greenhouse, the fella was on the phone, just in the alley between the gardens there, and I don't like to eavesdrop, but you can't help but hear sometimes, can you?'

She ran her finger down the page.

'He said: Mr Salt – not you, I assume.' Flashed a look up at me, went back to reading. 'Mr Salt, I'll be going ahead with it on Wednesday evening. Send the ring to Warrester. Thanks for all your help with this. Perfect… send the ring to Warrester.'

9. The Hard Shoulder

At the end of my dream I was in Jack Dixon's chair, eating undercooked chips, telling his widow I'd come to visit if she promised to wear that nasty little thong again.

When I woke up I was forty miles below Birmingham, and there was a vibrating pain in my back and an HGV with a broken fan belt speeding past in case that hadn't done the job.

My mouth tasted like yellow milk. I opened the window and threw out the whiskey bottle, sealed it back up.

In the ashtray in the door there was enough tobacco to roll a cigarette, but I didn't have papers or filters, and the car's lighter had a phone charger melted into it.

My head hurt. I took out the phone from behind me and checked it hadn't been Sarah calling, then I went back to sleep.

I hadn't told my dad that Sarah left me because I didn't want him to worry, and he always worried. There had been disappointments before, and every time he'd picked up the pieces, but he was getting too old for that now. So was I.

He called again and I answered it. Asked me how I was and I lied, and I asked him the same and he lied too.

'Did you get the internet fixed then?'

'I'm still waiting for them to come around.'

'Bastards.'

There was a silence, which I was supposed to fill.

'How come you rang?'

'I just wanted to talk to you,' he said. I wished I had anything to say. 'Sarah okay?'

I gathered the ashtray tobacco and a decent amount of ash into a corner with my finger, took a petrol receipt out of the back pocket of my trousers. A magpie hopped along the metal barrier on the central reservation.

'She's fine. At work.' I said.

'Oh, I thought she finished at twelve on Wednesdays.'

Did she?

'Apparently not.'

I rolled a filterless cigarette, and pushed the lighter down as far as it could go and held it there.

'Earl was in hospital the other day.' His brother.

'Yeah?'

'Halloween. He gets up in the night with a stomach ache, and he goes downstairs, but Sophia and her boyfriend are in the front room, so he goes to the kitchen and he has a piece of toast and sits down.'

The car lighter started smoking, so I opened a window.

'About twenty minutes later he can't move, and he shouts Lisa down, and she calls the non-emergency number, and they tell them to call an ambulance. Sophia's boyfriend has to help them lift him into it as well, so he's dying of embarrassment.'

The lighter turned orange and I took it out and lit the cigarette, which burned three quarters of the way down one side and then went out. I got the end going again.

'Lisa goes with him in the ambulance, and he said she's stroking his head, and she says Is this helping? And he says No it's not fucking helping! And he can't move at all, and he thinks his stomach's going to explode. And when he gets there they pump him full of painkillers, and they're prepping him for surgery.'

'Surgery?'

'Exploratory stomach surgery. Are you smoking?'

'No, I've just got the window open – I'm on the hard shoulder.'

'What are you doing on the hard shoulder?'

'I'm on the phone. What happened to Earl?'

'He's lying in the bed, in the gown and everything, and he gets up and goes for a walk down the ward.' Now he's laughing. 'Has to lean against a wall for a second cos the painkillers are making him dizzy, and he feels this shifting inside him.'

'Jesus Christ.'

'You know what's coming don't you?'

'Trapped wind?'

'Fucking trapped wind.' For a few seconds he's laughing so hard it's gone ultrasonic. 'It goes on for a full minute, and then when it stops the pain's gone. Fucking trapped wind.'

'What a twat.'

'What a twat – that's what I said to him.'

He told me something else about how much the new Principal at his work was making, and then he asked me if they'd sent a contractor to assess the damp in the bathroom yet. I told him they hadn't, and I'd call them as soon as I had a minute. Same with BT.

'I'm just asking,' he said.

He asked a few more things. And then I told him I had another call coming in, and he said he loved me.

Pure chance another call came in.

'McGann,' he said. 'How's the investigation, man?'

'She was in the summerhouse.'

'Down in Cornwall?'

'Yeah, yeah – neighbour saw her arguing with a guy, dragged her in there, tied her up in the garage.'

'Jesus.'

'Left the day before yesterday.'

He took a drag, mused it over.

'Anything else to go—'

'Neighbour thought he was a new man.'

'Like a metrosexual?'

'No, no, like a fucking...like he's her new man.'

'Who ties her up in the garage?'

'Nah she's fucking senile.'

'Sounds like she's lost the plot man.'

'That's what I thought.'

Now the magpie was playing Chicken across three carriageways, and as much as you wanted to see him pop you had to respect how he backed himself.

Gigger said 'So where you headed?'

'Warrester. Old lady said she heard him speaking on the phone to a Mr Salt, so I'm guessing that's Sarah's dad. Said thanks for all your help. Send the ring to Warrester.'

'Send the ring to Warrester?'

'Yeah.'

'That'll be the ransom then. Did you say the kidnapper's thanked him for his help?'

'That's what she said.'

'Well that's a fuckin' strange one.'

Burned my lips on the end of whatever you could call what I was smoking, said 'You don't think her dad's involved?'

'Well I was trying to think of what else it could be, man... Send us the ring, thanks very much. Sounds every bit like an inside job. I'm trying to think are we coming at it from the wrong angle?'

'Why would her dad want her kidnapped?'

'Why *would* her dad want her kidnapped...' He took another drag. 'Well let's say – and this is just speculation, cos like I said before it's no good biassing the investigation – but let's just say he's in a bit of money trouble.'

'Her dad?'

'Aye, her old man. Let's say he's had a couple of deals go bad, made a few dodgy bets out in Switzerland or something. Needs some money fast to cover his losses. And let's say his wife's got a diamond ring that's insured for 200 grand.'

'She had a load of crazy jewellery.'

'Okay, so if you call in a robbery, the police'll be all over you – in your house, checking your cameras, your bank accounts, phone calls.'

'Too risky.'

'Kidnapping's a different plate of pancakes, man.'

'Cos it's all done in advance.'

'Spot on. Tell the insurance you didn't call the police cos they'd have killed the hostage. They get you to phone it in and the police don't pile any resources into it because everyone's safe by then and you're a respectable member of society. Kidnapper keeps the ring, he's home and clear. Insurance pays out the 200 k and the fat lad pays off his debts.'

'What about Sarah?'

Too long a pause.

'Gig?'

'Now I'm speculating here. Speculating based on true crime and CSI and stuff I've seen online, so you've to take it with a pinch of salt.' He exhaled into the receiver and it boomed through my ear drum. 'When the police speak to Sarah, they're gonna know straight away if she was in on it, because they know how traumatic getting kidnapped is. Ah'd say if – *if* – it is her parents, and they've done their research, there's no chance they'd let Sarah in on the scam.'

I said 'She wouldn't have any part in it—'

He said 'And then there's something else… Based on everything I've seen, the police are gonna want some sort of physical evidence.'

'What does that mean?'

'It means if Sarah looks like she just walked out of a Miss Black Country contest, they're gonna be suspicious as hell.'

'So what, they'll want a black eye, bruises?'

'Fingers.'

I saw the bloody sheets rolled up in the garage.

'Fingers?'

'Fingers or toes.'

'Well which?'

Too short a pause.

'Ah'd have her fingers.'

I turned the key.

'I've gotta go, Gig. He said something about Wednesday night. I'll speak to you later.'

He said something else, but I was already gone.

10. The Rabbit

There was a lump of sick somewhere between my throat and my stomach that made it hurt to swallow, so I wasn't swallowing. It was something that had come and gone from week to week since I'd started smoking full-time, along with filthy coughs, unsatisfying breaths, and pick 'n' mix phlegm. This time though the tinge of iron in the taste of it suggested Mrs Dixon and her inch-thick pressure cooker were partly culpable.

I went the wrong way up two slip roads and ended up on the B-something-something, had to ask a little girl on a scooter for directions back to the motorway, which her mother didn't like. Now Warrester was signposted, and I half recognised the roads from a couple of days out with my dad when the child locks were on in the back of his 440 Volvo.

I spat a mouthful of saliva out of the window, which again the mother didn't appreciate.

These were the kind of country roads where the hedges had windmill cafés behind them, or a first sight of the sea after five hours in holiday traffic. Warrester didn't have a windmill café, and it was probably a hundred miles from the coast any way you went. All Warrester had was a green soup river, lined with million pound monuments to scumbags who didn't want anybody else to get a good look at it. And more pubs than people.

What Gigger said about Sarah's family fit too well to not be true.

When we lost Pound Road I read a text on her lockscreen. Her dad said he was concerned. Told her to come and stay, relax, and he could lend her some money to restart somewhere else.

He wanted her in his debt, under control. The ringmaster. Wanted her to trade and sell, and he couldn't stand the idea she wasn't his. Like Lucy, like even her mom who played the innocent. All of them.

They called it love and Sarah told herself it was too. And the more they hurt her here, the more she'd love them if they got away with it.

I was stressed, and I had this image of the bloody sheets clattering around and the New Man trying to cut her fingers off, and I was going too fast holding my horn down around bends when a rabbit flew out of one of the hedges and cut me off.

I hammered at the horn but it kept running.

'Ah!' I shouted at it, but it couldn't hear or it wouldn't listen. 'AH!'

It was at least fifteen under the limit. I tried to go around, but every time I swerved out it cut me off again and stayed in front.

I spat my mouth clear and got some of the sick out too,

which dragged a salmon colour across the back window.

'Out the fucking way!' I accelerated at it, but it had pace to burn and broke away again, with its dandelion tail flashing up and down teasing me. The road tightened into a chicane and the rabbit hugged the insides. I went to go around again but a Mazda pulled out of a junction right as I did, and I heard its smug little snigger when I backed off.

I eased further back so I could get more of a run. We'd gone almost a mile and I could see it starting to flag. The sick was bubbling now, and I felt as if there was no blood in my face. It turned back and looked at me again over its shoulder, and it flicked its eyebrows to goad me.

We were coming up to a hump in the road when I put my foot down again, and it kicked again, but I wasn't backing down this time. I feigned to go right and it bought the dummy and let me get alongside it on the left.

'You think you're better than me?' I asked it, trying to not dribble on my shirt, racing to the top of the hump. 'Think I don't know what you are?' And it looked at me surprised. And it stopped dead. And then it got hit by a white van bombing over the other side.

The tires screeched at the shock of the bang. Van lipped up onto the grass and scraped along the hedge, and then it straightened up and carried on driving like nothing happened.

I slammed the brakes and stopped and climbed across and out.

I shouted, but they didn't listen, kept bombing away.

The cow shit air was laced with burned rubber. I choked on it and spat some sick.

Ran back to the top of the hump, but there was no rabbit. Stepped out the way of a Winson Green mini-bus.

A bi-plane crossed the road and landed over in a field I couldn't see, and then it started up buzzing again and came back into the sky.

I threw up over some wild flowers.

No rabbit.

The buzzing and now some hot and cold sweat from the running and the sick were working together to make it hard to focus my eyes.

I had to find him.

Went to the hedges and got down and lifted up the knot of branches that sagged over the single yellow. There was an empty bottle of red wine and a broken button-bracelet, and further down the grill from a disposable barbecue. No rabbit.

I made the tutting noise that the woman downstairs did when she was trying to get the cats' attention, but I could barely hear it myself over the sound of the plane.

'Where are you?' I said, but nothing answered.

A man with a white moustache looked at me strange through his glasses and the windscreen of a Golf, and I picked up the bottle of wine and jabbed it towards his car and he drove off fast.

I followed the tracks that the tyres had left in the road, looking for blood. The plane went down to land again.

'You alright love?' A woman leaned out of the window of her Prius. She had a smear of toothpaste in the corner of her mouth. 'You okay, my love?'

'Go around.'

'You sure? You look a bit pale.' She looked down at the wine bottle. 'Have you had a crash?'

'I'm fine, just go around,' I told her again.

'Do you need me to call anyone love? I think you've had a cra—'

'I haven't had a fucking crash, I've murdered a fucking bunny rabbit! He's dead and he's vanished and I'm in a fucking hurry and I can look after myself, so will you FUCK OFF AND FUCKING GO AROUND!'

She went around, and I waited for her to put some distance between us and then I levelled off a pothole with the last of the sick.

Sat down next to it, and yesterday's rain started to seep through the seat of my trousers. My face felt better already, and my vision was cleaner.

I had a good look at the belly of the plane floating over me. It was a joyless yellow and white, and the wings were chequered in black and grey. I watched it turn around in a big circle and go over my head a couple of times.

There didn't seem much wrong with what was in the sick, the colour aside, and after a few deep ones I levered myself up onto a knee. That's when I saw the rabbit. Lying under the lip of dirt that the van swerved onto, hidden in the overhang of the grass. He was tiny. And he was shaking, barely breathing. One of his back legs and his tail had been crushed completely, and the skin on his stomach had been torn away and he was bleeding a hell of a lot.

I put down the wine bottle and got down on my front in the road beside him. His eye looked panicked but his body couldn't do anything about it. I pushed back some of the grass, and tried to think of something to say to him. I wanted to tell him that everything was going to be okay, but there were enough lies.

I put my cheek down against the tarmac, and I looked him in the eye, and I moved my hand up slowly so to not scare him, and stroked my thumb and my finger against his little ear. He stopped shaking, and in a few seconds his breathing slowed down.

The blood matted in his hair and made the grey a dirty purple, and where it was all torn away the muscle around his hip spasmed like it was trying to push out through the gap. The same purple ran out into a pool around him, and streams of it trickled over towards my face, but I didn't move because I didn't want to startle him.

I thought about breaking his neck, but I didn't know how I could do it without hurting him more first, and I didn't want to hurt him any more. Thought about doing him in with Syn, but it didn't feel right to leave him all ruined on his own even for any time at all.

Cars slowed to go around me, and some sped up too. The bi-plane had dropped out of the air at some point and it hadn't started up again this time. I didn't know how long it had all taken, but now I had to see it through.

His breathing got strained, like his lungs weren't filling up anymore. I stroked him slowly, as softly as I could. He looked glazed and hazy, and after a while the muscle stopped spasming, and he was calm. His eye lifted up gently to look at mine, and I took my hand away from him and left it down by my side.

'All better,' I told him.

He went for one more breath and he missed it, and then he was dead.

I stayed with him for a while, and pulled out some of the long grass from beneath the hedge to cover him with, and then I went and got back in the car.

11. The Empty Shelves

Sarah did love her parents, and her dad hated me. He hated how I dressed, he hated how I didn't talk to him like he shit bubblegum, and he hated that I beat him at mini-golf in Llandudno on his wife's birthday weekend.

He did something to do with stock markets, or he'd made a lot of money trading private equity shares if that's not the same thing. He was bald but he had a tattoo treatment that made it look like he shaved his head, and his nose was red and full of indentations with black hairs growing out of them.

'I'm Mr Salt,' he said to me when we first met, outside a restaurant he'd chosen because it was too expensive for me to offer to pay, and because they specialised in some sort of basically raw steak he knew I wouldn't eat. I told him I'd be Mr McGann then, but he just didn't speak to me.

We'd turned up late because Sarah put her foot through her only pair of black tights and we had to find a place that sold them at seven on a Sunday evening. He didn't like that one bit.

Around me in the fields people wrenched horses over fences.

Salt wanted me out of the picture. Sent the Hammer Man to do the job. He knew what I'd do if he gave me the chance.

The sign said *Welcome to Warrester*, and the flowers in the roundabout said *PLEASE DRIVE SLOWLY* in all different colours.

I went straight over, and the road dipped down to where the high street started and turned into cobbles. Syn didn't like cobbles.

The cheap plastic signs glued onto old stone shops looked great, and the locals' faces looked like they knew it.

I needed a mint for the sick taste.

Further down, the road forked around an old church, and in the front garden some old sour-looking samaritan plucked crisp packets into a carrier bag and handed out dirty looks. I gave her one back but the turbulence from the cobbles undermined it.

The signs said the car parks were way down by the river. I bounced Syn up halfway on the pavement where the road widened a few feet, climbed out, locked up, and went into a place called Jenny's News.

A bell rang and a man with a fluorescent pink turban came through a curtain of hanging beads and sat down behind the counter. It was empty – spaces all over the shelves, nothing much in the way of fruit or veg. I went to the fridge.

It occurred to me that I needed to start asking questions, and that shopkeepers were as good a place as any. But I had to be careful too – anyone could be in Salt's pocket, so I had to act as if everyone was. The questions – the interrogations – had to be inconspicuous, general.

I wanted chocolate milk, but all they had were the 300 mil kids' shit.

'You Jenny?' I said to the guy. He was pretending to read the entertainment pages. When he looked up at me his head jerked backwards like he recognised me, but then he thought about the question and tried to smooth it over.

He had a semi-skimmed Indian accent, said 'Jenny's dead. Sold it.'

I wondered about her, took a can of dandelion and burdock and a bottle of the brown stuff, turned back to him, walked over.

'Shame. How long you been here, then?'

'Two year.'

'Huh.' I looked at the scratch cards. I'd won eighteen pounds the second time I ever bought one, on my sixteenth birthday. Since then things had been dry. Around New Jenny's mouth there was a smear of toothpaste. I rubbed my eye to see if it came off, put the things on the desk and he rang them up and the price flashed on the screen.

'This chocolate milk.' I gestured to it but he didn't look down, kept his eyes on me, looked maybe on edge, which could have been the way he looked anyway. 'Don't you ever get in any of the bigger ones? The glass bottles, or the cartons?'

'No,' he said. He didn't like me, but I was starting to like how honest he was being about that.

Anyway I was going somewhere with this.

'Guess the fresh stuff's higher risk? Milk, apples.'

He didn't respond. The price on the screen was more than I'd expected it to be.

I said 'It's the thing with these big supermarkets, you know? They can have everything, throw it all out if it doesn't sell. Doesn't hurt them.'

He was nodding his head slowly now. That gave me a little buzz. I was so in control, thinking fast and talking slow.

'I saw a couple up the road there – the Sainsbury's, Waitrose.'

He nodded.

I said 'Yeah. Yeah well I say we could do with more people like Jenny – like you. Real people. I'll take a number nine too. That one, yeah.' He rang it up. I hadn't clocked it was a two pounder, but the sale was lubricant. I had to keep him going. 'They don't all feel like that now though do they? The ones with the money.'

'Three seventy-nine, please.' He stood up slowly as he said it, and partly because of the turban and partly because of how tall he was anyway, he loomed over me and it was like we were too close together, but I wasn't going to step back – I was too cool.

Sarah said I could be manipulative, I said manipulative's an ugly word – if nobody's getting hurt, it's not manipulation, it's persuasion. Like she persuaded me to move away from where my dad lived, to a part of town where we couldn't afford the two-bed semi even before I lost my job. Like she persuaded me to buy a car so we didn't have to get the bus to work anymore. She made me want to do those things, because I wanted to do what she liked, make her happy. Be around her. She got those things, I got her. That's persuasion.

I said 'Of course,' and I put my hands in my pockets and tried to separate the coins and the keys, and I realised that none of these things were coins. It was all in the car again. In the CD holder. Something about the way he was looking at me told me somehow he'd known that all along.

Jesus, this guy was huge. Arms like beer kegs. Where did everyone find the time to make themselves look like that? I had to keep talking.

'You see them – you know – like I saw them on the way through, the cars out the front of those places. These rich people in their four-by-fours, and –'

'You have no money?' he asked, but really it sounded more like a statement.

I went through my keys again.

'Look I left it in the car—'

'Out!' he said, and he pointed at the door. This was crazy now. Jenny was going crazy. His business was tanking, sure, that'd make everyone turn a little, but I wasn't the enemy. I mean who the hell was this guy? Who did he think I was? Or did he know? Did he know who I was?

'Look,' I said, and he stepped back like he flinched. And I said 'Pal,' but he just kept going backwards, and he lost all his height, and now he was scrambling in his pockets and I didn't like the look of that. I got one of my shins up on the counter and I caught the milk and it hit the floor and went rolling down towards him, and I was getting the other one over when he pulled out his phone, and he was shouting for me to stop. Now the doorbell rang, and the two of us watched a man in heeled boots and an overcoat come through and look at us, then slip it into reverse.

I waited for the door to close.

'Who? Who are you calling?!' I said. Raised my voice now.

'Police! Go! Go! I'll call the police!' He was less stern now, shaking a little. I'd gone in control again. He was halfway covered by the curtain beads, and he was showing me his phone, and it was calling nine nine nine. I was totally relaxed. I wanted a cigarette. I got my other shin up and reached and slid the tobacco door over, took a pack from the shelves, flicked one out and lit it.

'Police, police,' he said into the phone or to me. Both.

'Where is it?' I said, back to regular volume. 'The Jaguar.'

He told me he had no idea. Told me he didn't want trouble.

I stayed with him for a minute. Smoked and watched him while he gave his address to the police. It all seemed pretty convincing. I mulled over my interrogating technique. Almost asked him what he thought – what I might work on. Then I got down and went out. Jenny hadn't seen anything worth my while. They had him beaten down.

I felt good again now, felt like I'd had a sombre morning but now I was making ground again. I'd needed that – exchange with a guy wound too tight. Yeah. Made me feel like I was going in the right direction myself in grabbing some things by the horns, you know?

I finished my cigarette and dropped it first time down into a drain without it touching the sides. Today was going to be a good day. Get out the cage. I could feel the red stuff running through me, and a little still maybe at the back of my throat. Got in the car.

'Hey jackass!' the call went out, and I sucked in a breath and closed my eyes to soak it in. There was a crowd of old women trailed around my car, wearing shawls pulling tartan trolleys. 'It's a fucking bus stop. You can't park in a bus stop.'

I wound down my window so I could hear him clearer – the driver – short sleeve blue shirt, village people leather gloves. I was the madman. The ladies finished filing in and he could see me.

He said 'It's business access only here,' and I turned to him, and he did the same thing Jenny did – the little flinch

– and I just looked at him, and he pressed the button that folded the doors shut and we watched each other for a second through them, and then he pissed off.

He was right. I looked down at the yellow markings and up at the signs. With the chance of the police coming to investigate the disturbance at the newsagent's I couldn't be too careful. I wound the window and hooked Syn around and up a hill, looking for somewhere discreet to leave her, all the time with another eye out for the Jag on a driveway.

12. The Two Magpies

About the only place that wasn't Residents Only was a pub: The Two Magpies, part of a mile up the hill. Sign looked like fresh paint. On it one bird wore a pink bonnet and the other a top-hat. Bonnet stood upright on the branch and the other one hung upside down off it. I wondered if they put it up the wrong way around, because the bonnet had a string to keep it on and the top-hat didn't.

Wasn't sure if I clipped one of the picnic benches on the back car park, but then a woman came out and I was pretty sure I did so I was hiding under the steering wheel.

She had brown skin and brown hair with blonde ends, and she was wearing red Reebok trainers and purple jeans with a hole in one of the knees. She looked around and fixed on the car for a second, and then took a case of cigarettes out of her coat pocket and started smoking one. Didn't seem to notice me. She sat on one of the benches without wiping it dry or anything.

I got my jacket from the back seat and put it on, made

sure I had my wallet and the photo and my phone, and then I squeezed the working door handle until it popped, but I didn't open it yet.

She didn't look like she smoked. There are thirteen-year-old girls who look okay with the first one in their hand and fifty-year-old women on twenty-a-day who just can't pull it off. Luck of the draw.

I wanted to get around her in some way where she wouldn't make me move Syn. Maybe I could have waited for her to finish smoking, but the kidnappers wouldn't be waiting to cut Sarah's fingers off – Sarah couldn't wait. And anyway I didn't like waiting.

I eased open the door and slipped out, keeping down low behind it. The surface was crumbling asphalt, not made for discreet getaways. I took off my shoes again and got my hands dirty doing it, took off my socks too because it didn't make sense to make a mess of them as well. I put the socks over my hands and held the shoes. Her cigarette was barely started, like she wasn't interested in smoking it – just wanted something to admire. I pushed the door to and turned the key and stayed down low.

At Pound Road we smoked the air blue and the walls grey, and we painted and scrubbed and bleached it down, but nothing beat it.

When we moved to the flat, Sarah quit cold turkey, told me she could see the fridge and the washing machine turning yellow and the same was happening to my lungs.

I didn't listen.

So the girl in the Reeboks was about thirty feet from me, half facing the exit I needed, half facing the door she came out through. Really how she hadn't heard me so far I didn't know, but there wasn't time to think about it. I figured my best chance was to stay close up to the fence and go slowly and not make eye contact, so that was what I was doing when she saw me and made a run for the doors saying 'Fuck fuck fuck fuck fuck fuck.'

I called over to her but she was in a real hurry trying to get the door open, and it jammed somehow so I started running myself, waving, trying to get her to calm down, and she was just saying Jesus fucking Christ.

When I got to her she let go of the handle and she was just looking at me with these big brown eyes, and she stepped back as far as the wall let her, and she put her hands to her ears and pulled out these little wireless earphones she'd had in.

First I asked her if I could finish off her cigarette, and then when she unfroze and gave me that and I noticed she was wearing a staff black polo, I asked if we could go inside and get something to drink.

She poured me a chocolate milk and said it was on her, which was nice. Still she was looking at me strangely – a lot like the bus driver and like Jenny did – and I didn't understand fully why, but I'd really needed some energy and I'd left the other things at the newsagents, so for now I was just enjoying my milk.

'I didn't mean to startle you,' I told her. 'That's why I took my shoes off.'

'You took your shoes off so I didn't think it was weird?'

Her lipstick was red to match her Reeboks.

'Well I wanted to be discreet.'

'Discreet?' She looked down at the sock-gloves. I screwed them off and started putting them back on my feet. She told me to hang on and tore me off some blue roll to wipe everything with first.

'Nobody looks good when they get caught being discreet,' I said. She poured me another glass.

The pub was warm and the carpet was thicker than any duvet I ever slept with. The walls were a pistachio colour. Smelled like they'd had a new coat, looked like they hadn't in decades.

I felt like curling up over by the fire, but then I thought of Sarah. Now when I thought of her my head started throbbing, or at least I remembered how much it hurt already.

'What's your name then?' said the woman, looking a little less afraid of me now, but still standing back at the distance limit for a two-way conversation.

I didn't like the idea of telling her who I was. Anonymity gave me freedom, kept me safe. On the other hand, this was good chocolate milk — a free, cold glass of chocolate milk. Hardly the calling card of a kidnapper's accomplice.

And there was a weight of lies, and it wasn't really clear how far they'd got me. Even Dixon only really gave it up when she'd worked me out. People didn't like being lied to. People liked being listened to — grin along while they ooze out whatever dull wank's dribbled together in their brain that day, and get on the carousel so they can drag you through how it reinforces the other three things they're always talking about.

Sarah said I never listened. Never listened. Obviously wasn't true, but how many times can you be bothered to agree with something you know they'll never do anything about?

The way her family treated her was a top five topic for discussion, but it wasn't up for debate because she didn't like what I had to say about them, so I sat and nodded along and now they'd taken her hostage and they were going to cut her fingers off.

It wasn't really about listening – it was about active listening, assertive listening. About listening and then doing something about what you've heard, whether they want you to or not.

When I got her free I'd listen again, and I'd get her safe, and I'd find her dad, and I'd make the cunt swing for what he'd done to her.

'You're not telling me?' she said.

I didn't know how long I hadn't spoken for.

'Marco.'

'Marco?'

'Yeah.'

'That's a nice name.' She was pouring herself a cup of tea, never turning her back fully on me. She gestured to offer me some, but I tapped the milk to say I was okay. 'So, Marco,' I straightened my shoulders, sipped at my drink, listened. 'Is it your blood?' That caught me by surprise, and I think she could tell it did. 'On your face. Is it your blood on your face?'

I looked in the mirror behind the spirits, quickly, so she might not notice. Tommy Lee Jones, *Batman Forever*. With all the morning's action I'd forgotten totally about putting my face down in a pool of rabbit blood. Now it was dry and starting to flake off, which if anything had made me look more menacing. Explained a few things.

I looked back down at my milk and took another go on it.

There was no-one else in the place.

'How about this,' I said, 'you get a question, then I get a question.' She was getting the normal milk out of the fridge now. 'When one of us has heard enough, conversation ends.'

I could tell she liked it. Who wouldn't – she was getting paid to be here. Now I had her convinced I wasn't a serial killer it was just a strange day at work to break the monotone.

I had half my right sock on, none of the left, and the carpet felt like the back of a cat between my toes.

'Okay, so question one – the blood,' she said.

'The blood belonged to a rabbit. I was an accessory to his murder in the early hours of the morning. I put my face in the blood to be a comfort in his final seconds. My question.' She drank some tea, smiling and trying to work out if I was kidding. 'You work in this pub—'

'Yes! What do you do?'

'Woah, wait – that wasn't the question.'

'It was *a* question. Now answer mine.'

She was fast. Was she hiding something? Who wasn't.

'Electrical logistics. System management.'

'Computers?'

'Yes. Two questions for me.' I was faster. She laughed. Now she was leaning on her hands on the bar. 'Ever seen an F-Type Jaguar around here? Or maybe an XK or something like that.'

She thought about accusing me of a double question but the mystery had her hooked. She looked out of the window over my shoulder and considered it. She was serious, and I liked that.

'An F-Type?' she asked.

I nodded.

'There are a lot of nice cars around here.'

I said 'Anyone you know?' and I thought I might have seemed a little tense because she drew back again, but then I registered the old guy she'd seen walk in. He had hunched shoulders and a green coat. He hung up the coat on the stand and came to the bar and ordered stout, and she said good morning, and the guy, Bruce, told her it was the afternoon. I didn't like that. I put my left sock on for something to do, and Bruce went and sat in the corner by the window and read the *Beano*.

She said 'I'm trying to think. Nobody who drinks here. Usually the rich boys drink down by the river with the tourists. And there are posh houses all over the place. It's a weird question. Why?'

'I'm looking for one.'

She laughed again, and her cheeks bunched around her eyes like Jack Nicholson's. She said 'Your Turbo does look a bit beaten up.' She wet a piece of blue roll in the sink, came over and handed it to me and I started on getting my face clean.

'It's not the car I'm looking for,' I said.

'Oh.' Her face relaxed back into place. 'So what then, Marco? What are you looking for?'

Bruce was choking on something good.

'You asked too many questions,' I said, and I finished the milk like I had the first one. I took out my cigarettes and she said she'd come out too. Bruce could pour his own.

We went around to the front and looked over what we could see of the river and the peaks behind it. It was a cold day and something had irritated my right nipple.

She was looking at the lump on my head probably, and she said 'You look like you've been in a fight.'

I said 'I have,' and she smiled like I was kidding.

I said I liked the sign, and she said she painted it herself so I didn't push her on the top-hat. I told her about the bus driver, and she called them bastards. She said it was a good thing that fewer cars ran through the centre, but the private car parks by the river were way overpriced.

'I'm sorry I wasn't more help,' she said.

'You were. Free car park, free chocolate milk.'

She stepped around in front of me and checked I got all of the blood off. And I said yeah that too and she smiled.

She said 'If I were you, I'd ask Mrs Thatcher, down at the Post Office.'

'Thatcher?'

'Yeah. She knows everyone in Warrester – everyone who uses the Post Office. Been here for fifty years. She's a bit deaf, and she'll talk your ear off, but she knows her cars.'

I got a video game checkpoint buzz and my stomach folded over itself. And she saw I was going to leave but she told me to wait there just a second. I wondered if she was calling the police. Thought about running. I was standing on the wall on the edge of jumping off it when she came back wheeling a purple bike with a D-lock around the handlebars.

'As long as you promise to bring it back,' she said, and she leaned it towards me and I took it by the saddle. I didn't know what to say. I thought I might ask her why, but I felt stupid, so I just said thanks. She told me not to worry about it, and that she got off shift at ten so if she could have it back by then then that'd be cool. On the frame it said RACER, and above that OLIVIA.

She told me she called it Liv.

I swung my leg over. It had been a long time since I rode a bike and Liv was made for smaller shoes, but it was a crazy gesture and with not much to go on I was going to have to cover a lot of ground if I wanted to catch the Jag.

I flicked my cigarette at another drain and it went down again.

'Good luck,' she said.

13. The Green Jaguar

The bike rattled like she wanted to be a unicycle, her front tyre was buckled so the brake-pad only touched the wheel once every rotation, and if anyone got a good look at what the saddle was doing to me we'd both be arrested.

I saw the litter woman still down at the church and made a beeline, nearly came off on the cobbles saluting.

With the blood gone from my face and a few shots of milk in my belly I was bulletproof.

Everyone said we were inseparable, me and Sarah. We worked together, slept together, showered together. We had this game when we brushed our teeth, where when one stopped brushing the other had to stop within three seconds or swallow their toothpaste.

I hadn't brushed my teeth in three months.

The thing was she felt trapped, and our relationship was the only thing she had enough control over to change. And what I hadn't done was react – get her away from her family, out of Rhoder & Dalt, into a place where she felt like she could change things, where she felt like she was free.

I gunned it along the cobbles, and the cold and the wind made my eyes water.

Where the Post Office was wasn't obvious. I thought about asking at the church, but I didn't have time to listen to them. There was a closed sign in Jenny's door. Some people don't have what it takes to survive.

I did a couple more lengths of the high street, which wasn't all that big, then got off and locked Liv to a one way sign, zipped my jacket up and walked.

There were less people on the street than earlier. Gone home for some cake and a nap and the news.

Eventually, at the top of the street by the roundabout, I saw the place where the Post Office used to be. The lump on the back of my head twinged and the shock pulsed through my face. The signs had been taken down, but the cutout of the old red van was still in the window, and it had snow and tinsel on top of it, and in the front seat there was Father Christmas with his shirt untucked and his cheeks all red like he'd left his wife and had a few pints before work.

There was a handwritten note on the door with some lengthy number code in the corner. It said something like: *We've moved over into the Nisa across the road. Sorry about the inconvenience. Phyllis Thatcher.* I turned around and saw the sign in the Nisa window, buried behind special offers.

Crossed over and went in. There was no-one at the front desk. Thatcher was at the back but she didn't know I was until I went around to the side of the glass and really hammered it.

'Ooh sorry my love. Just a minute,' she said, and I went back around and waited at the window while she finished off in a filing cabinet and made a meal of climbing down from her stool. People lived longer than they were supposed to.

The thirty-year-old computer on her desk said it was twelve-fifty-nine.

'What?' I asked – she'd said something but it was garbled and I'd missed it.

'Sorry dear?'

'What did you say?'

'Oh – I said we're not sending you off are we?'

I had no idea what she was talking about.

'You're Mrs Thatcher, yes?'

'Yes that's me dear,' she said.

I had my face pressed against the microphone and she had her ear against the receiver, and I still had to raise my voice.

'The woman at The Two Magpies says you might be able to help me,' I told her.

Behind me a man in a white coat considered which of the cauliflowers he was fingering was fresher. I never saw the attraction of a cauliflower, but Sarah said peas weren't enough. She said I looked unwell most of the time. Malnourished.

'Lovely girl – always comes in for a chat. Lovely girl.'

'Yes. Look can you help me? I need information, quickly.'

She was squinting her eyes to make her ears work better. 'I am sorry my love, I didn't catch that.'

'Okay—'

'I'm a bit hard of hearing,' she said. I waited for her to get her ear back onto the mic. The man in the white coat was standing behind me now. He'd abandoned the cauliflower altogether and decided it was stamps he needed.

'Okay.' I was shouting now. 'Who do you know in Warrester that owns a Jaguar?'

'A what?'

'A Jaguar. The car.' I mimed driving, and she looked like she got it.

'Oh a Jaguar.' She was playing with a book of second class stamps, peeling one off at the corner and then smoothing it back down with her nails. 'Well, let me think,' she said, and then she mumbled something again.

'What?'

'Is it the F-Type, my love?'

'Yes!' I said. Got me excited. Wanted to tell her about it – the Hammer Man, Lucy, Tuppence, Dixon. Wanted to sit in the car with her, tell her I wasn't the same and I wasn't like her family, and we were going to Paris.

'Course they all park by the river now, love. Alan!' Alan came out of the back door carrying two hot cups of tea and a cafetiere. He was about five feet three and had on glasses and a moustache. Put one down on her desk.

'Alan!' she shouted again. This one startled him and he spilled half of his tea on a notebook, and that made her jump and she knocked hers clean off, all over the crotch of Alan's trousers. I couldn't work out if he was completely oblivious or just hardened by historical scalding, but he didn't seem troubled by it. He put the cafetiere down, rested his hand on the shoulder of her knitted blue cardigan.

'How can I help you my love?' he said to her. Their voices sounded the same, and they both turned their heads to the side and pulled straining faces when the other was talking.

'This young man wants to know who drives the F-Type around the town here.'

'The F-Type eh? Powerful piece of kit that, my love.'

'Four point one to sixty,' she said.

He said 'The V8 does, dear, but not the V6. And that's just the point – if memory serves, there are at least two such beasts in the vicinity.' The pace and the volume of the conversation was entrancing. 'Which one's the lad looking for?'

I realised that they were both looking at me now, both tilting towards an ear.

'Either,' I said, but that wasn't going to be enough – they needed a reason. People always needed a reason, even to just bother to think about something. 'I want to buy one.'

The two of them went back to one another, and they said 'Let me think' at the same time, or only one of them said it and the other just moved their lips.

The phone at the front of the shop started ringing but there was no-one there to answer it so it gave up.

'Tall fellow,' said Thatcher. 'Black hair.'

'Him just off Washway – what they call the bypass now of course.' The second part was for me.

'That's him. Herring Close.' She was back working at the stamp book, and she plucked one off with a little vigour when her brain clicked into gear – 'Forty-two – because he lives next to Mr Walters.'

'That's right,' Alan confirmed. 'Now if I'm remembering rightly, that's the V6 – sounds like the old E-type.'

'That's right,' she agreed. 'If I were the lad that'd be the one I'd splash for.' She turned to me and got down to her mic, and said 'Five point five to sixty, love, but you'll save on fuel, and it'll be a fair whack cheaper in the first place.' It wasn't how I'd thought this was going to go.

Now I was routing through my pockets for a piece of paper and a pen to write it all down on, but Alan already had that covered. He passed the address underneath the window on a post-it note. Either it had been his handwriting on the door too or they just had two halves of the same brain. I put it in my pocket.

'The name?' I said.

'The name, dear?' said Thatcher, looking puzzled.

'Of the man on Herring Close.'

They turned to look at one another like they had a better chance of finding something in the other's head than they did their own. Alan stroked his moustache.

'I can't think that it's ever come up,' he said. He went back to Thatcher, said 'Unless anyone's mentioned him… I can't remember anything on the return.'

'Well I was just trying to think really.' She did some more thinking, then she told me that the people that she knew by name were usually the ones who popped in for a chat. This one she could only have seen a couple of times, to her knowledge, and didn't talk much. A private man, as far as she could tell.

'Course he could just be shy,' Alan interjected.

'Very true Alan,' she said. 'He keeps me honest.'

Behind me the man in the white coat shifted his balance. He was tapping one of his feet in a heartbeat on the floor. For a second I watched his reflection in the glass. Seemed to be staring directly at the back of my head.

'The V8, my love,' Thatcher said – the skin on her neck swung when her jaw moved – 'now the V8's a different creature. Have you driven one before?'

'Yes.' I nodded, and her left eye narrowed but then it opened up again.

She said 'They say the V8 can hit 200.'

Alan said that he was sceptical of that in real terms.

I had some phlegm caught in the back of my throat that

tasted like chocolate. Zoned out trying to dislodge it, and had to rebuild what Alan had been saying. Something about the river.

Listen.

'What? I'm sorry, what?'

Alan adjusted his hearing aid and moved in closer to the mic.

He backtracked, 'I said, funnily enough the other fellow seems relatively aloof as well. I don't think he uses us here. Some people go closer to work if it's easier, and course there's quite a few who use the other companies now.'

'But we've seen him, and we've definitely heard him,' Thatcher told me, 'and I don't hear like I used to, you know, so that tells you how loud he is.' She picked up Alan's cup from the desk, looked around for hers and couldn't find it so drank his.

'Could be a woman too, son. Tinted windows,' he added.

'Drives like a bloke though love, if you know what I mean.'

Pulled her hand up from the stamps and made a wanker gesture. I mean that's what it looked like.

'Where?'

They looked at each other again.

'Mmm, down by the river usually, but everywhere really – tend to do twat-laps, you know,' she said. 'I couldn't specify an address.'

Alan picked up his teacup, looked suspicious at the pink lipstick mark around its rim.

He said 'You'll hear it though.'

'What?' Thatcher shouted at him.

'I said he'll hear it coming!'

'I know love, I was having you on,' she winked at me.

Alan feigned to give her the back of his hand. He said 'Funny how they both bought the same colour, isn't it?

Both British Racing Green, son.'

'They want all the bloody same as each other, love,' she told him. 'Excuse my French. Was that everything today my love? Couldn't interest you in some holiday insurance could I? Or a Costa coffee for three ninety-five?' The coffee machine over to my right smelled like drip-tray.

'No, thanks,' I said, and I said I had to leave. They said they hoped they'd see me again.

The man in the white coat was gone, and I wasn't sure he'd ever been there at all.

I picked up a Boost bar and a bottle of Lemon Lucozade. There was still no-one at the checkout so I left what I reckoned was a fair price on the counter, took the phone off the hook because it was ringing again, went to get the bike.

14. The Haunted House

I threw up between Greggs and Oxfam, dry-heaved for a while in an alley further down. Then I had the Boost and the Lucozade. Settled my stomach.

Rode up to the flower roundabout and crossed onto it.

In Oldon the roundabouts were filthy fly-tipping hotspots. The one outside Pound Road had a fridge in the middle for six months. Me and Sarah got drunk one night, went over with a pack of acrylics and painted bluebirds on the doors. She drew the beach on one side with these slashed orange clouds, and I drew us selling rabbits from a hut on the other. Two days later the council took it away.

In Warrester the roundabouts were cut like private golf courses, and this one had a triangle of fountains and the PLEASE DRIVE SLOWLY flower sign swooped through them.

I didn't want to jump the gun – things were still up in the air with the kidnapping – but now I felt closer to

Sarah than at any point in the last three months, and I'd never really bought her flowers before so picking some of these seemed a good way to show her things had changed.

For a minute I thought about whether I could make the sign say something else, but the nose full of chocolate milk sick hadn't put me in the right mindset. I uprooted the PLEASE because it was made up of reds and oranges and because they didn't mean it anyway.

I had this picture of us replanting them in pots at the flat, and later on the roundabout at Pound Road. For now I filled my back pockets with everything I could get, hoped it didn't compost on the saddle.

Washway – the bypass – was the first exit, downhill, lined with these high class birch trees.

There was a chance I remembered some of it from when I'd been here before, but the houses had changed in twenty years. Bigger now, greyer, and the gates had sharper spikes, and half of them had garage space for a family of four.

I looked for Herring Close, found the sign bolted to the outer wall of a place with salmon pink turrets.

Tied the bike to a tree and put my collar up and walked to forty-two.

It had a small garden gate and steps up to the door, and a concrete driveway big enough for two or three cars, but there was only one. Under a washed out blue cover, a gleaming Jaguar F-Type, in British Racing Green.

Fired me up.

At the summerhouse I'd let them get the drop on me. Not them, Dixon. It didn't matter who, it just couldn't happen again. I let her get behind me. Not this time.

The lump was thumping now and I slapped it until it stopped.

Looked over my shoulder, took the steps quickly, tried the door: black wooden giant with a gold lion knocker, and it opened, and for a second the whole atmosphere quaked, like it was going to collapse in on itself, and my ears popped and the pain in my head folded me over. And then whatever it was went away.

The door creaked forwards, let out this strange smell like someone was brewing beer.

Tiles on the floor looked like a chess board and dotted around there was a full set of these oversized black pieces – maybe a foot each.

I shut the dark in, reached for the knife, and knew by the feel of the sheath it was empty.

The lump throbbed.

Dixon, the old bitch. Or the cat. Or the man in the white coat. All of them.

Down behind the door there was the Queen, with a sharp crown like a bottle cap. I picked her up, couldn't believe how much she weighed.

I felt the compulsion again to call out Sarah's name, but I knew if I did he'd find me first – The Minotaur.

Somewhere in the beer there was the smell of lavender incense. Sarah liked incense – she used to buy it from the shop in the Corn Exchange in Holworth. When I saved her I'd buy her everything she wanted with what I had left of Gigger's money – the dream catchers, and the spices and the salts for her headaches. I'd said it was a waste, placebo crap, but it wasn't crap if it meant something to Sarah. If it meant something to Sarah, then it meant something to me.

A floorboard creaked and I raised the Queen.

It had come from somewhere deep into the house. Up the stairs, I was sure, and I wanted to go straight at it but I knew that wasn't the right move. If I found Sarah first, I could get her safe before I went back for him.

My usual wheezing was amplified by the dark in the hallway. I rounded the living-room door like a ghost and pushed it back into the frame.

The curtains were closed, and they were thick green blackouts, but still a little light came between them and the bay window. There were two oxblood leather settees, and they were pointed at a fifty-inch flatscreen. One of the curved ones.

No-one in the room but me.

In the corner he had a real fireplace like we always wanted, and butted up against the outside of the chimney breast there was an old looking wooden bookcase.

The smell of the incense followed me.

Karen Sortee, Amrit Nath, Domonic Burell. These were Sarah's books.

Floorboard creaked again. Directly above me. I was about to meet him. The New Man. The Minotaur.

In the corner of the room one of Sarah's boots looked a little small, but I recognised the scuff on the tartan tongue, and I reached for it to find her initials on the soul, and then through the dark, like a thousand miles away, locked up in the attic or a sealed vault, she screamed.

'MARCO!'

And again the walls shook and the books fell from the shelves, and the lump drummed through my head.

Dropped the shoe, took the Queen to the hallway, and I could hear him laughing – the same laugh from the phone. The ugly laugh.

And while my eyes readjusted to the almost pitch black I pointed them at the front door. And again I thought about running. Leaving Sarah. Whether I really wanted any of this. And I knew I couldn't live with myself.

'MARCO!' again, muffled. Then the laugh, then the drumming in the back of my head.

Took the stairs slow, and the dark subsided a little, and along the wall the picture frames filled with photographs. And they were photographs of me and her.

'There are no photos of us, Marco.'

The two of us sitting on our mattress on our first anniversary, and I was spreading raspberry jam on toast, and she was trying to get it off me because she hated crumbs in the bed. She had on her glasses, and I was in a pair of Y-fronts and this leopard print scarf she bought.

I kept going, pushed my hand and the Queen against my head so it didn't split in half.

The lavender thickened and the beer died away.

Next frame was carved into black flowers. I ran my finger up a stem, wiped out six years of dust.

'No photos of us, Marco.'

We'd gone to a Twenties party, and I wore a spinning bow tie and Sarah had a green headband with a peacock feather we found at the Botanical Gardens shooting out. She was standing behind me, and I was pulling a face but she wasn't talking to me because I'd pointed out she'd taken longer to get dressed than we'd spend at the party.

At the top of the stairs, between two of the doors, I could see a bigger picture. I walked on the insides of my feet and the outside of the stairs.

Again a creak. Not me, but this time not a floorboard either. This time maybe the click of an old chair. Handcuffs on a radiator, hammer of a forty-five.

And the bannister shook, and I tried to hold my ground, fumbled the Queen, got a grip of her and held on until it settled down.

Now with the landing in my eyeline I could see a pale light under the left door. Something like daylight. I crept up, begged the stairs not to rat me out, and the bigger picture came into focus.

'No photos.'

At the beach, on Tolten bay, and my shoulders poked through my towel like the prison spikes on playground fences, and Sarah bent double, laughing at the burned mess of my face.

I squeezed the two pieces of polaroid together in my pocket, made sure they were there.

In the distance, a girl and a boy, running naked towards the sea holding red sandcastle buckets, both of them blonde, and the ringlets in their hair skipped around them.

I took out the polaroid. Creased from my pocket. And I was trying to flatten it out, trying to match it up against this one that must have been a copy of it or something, when the keys clicked into the lock, and the front door came open, and the hallway and the stairs lit up.

Panicked, stopped dead, and then snapped through the door on the right, put it back where it came from.

'Dan?' called a woman's voice, but not Sarah's. 'Door's ope – ah ah ah – shoes off please mister. Looks like Daddy forgot too.'

The kids were shouting, but just like kids are always shouting. Garbled nonsense, but definitely no fear – not kidnap victims.

Something didn't add up. With the photos and the books and the boots.

'Get changed and I'll do you a jammy,' she said.

I looked around me at their neatly made beds and their matching teddies. I didn't know exactly how, but there was every chance I'd made an awful and very honest mistake, and it wasn't my fault the world wouldn't see it like that. My heart bled for innocent paedophiles everywhere, but I wasn't about to join them.

'Dan?' she called up again.

I had to get out. The kids were doing knots up the stairs. I looked for a closet for me and the Queen, but there were only little plastic drawers. The window didn't open except for the top part, which had like a child-latch.

I was ready to run. Pressed up against the door. I'd let it swing open, and then I'd be through it before the little bastards knew what hit them. Throw them down the stairs if that's what it needed.

Then another door clicked open. The Minotaur door. And the Minotaur went 'Rooooaaaaar!' and the kids screamed and they squealed because he had a hold of them, and they were laughing.

He had a soft voice. And he was asking how their days had gone, what they did, and I raised up the Queen, ready to bring it down on all of them. But the stairs were going in reverse now, and the voices receding, and eventually all four of them were talking at once below me, laughing at each other and clattering plates.

I let some air out of my lungs.

I had to move quickly. Got the door open. The landing light was on now and I could see the mud on the stairs was scandalous, and it was from the footprints and from the mulch in my pockets, so there were real clumps. I tucked the flowers deeper.

Tried the bathroom first. There was a basket of toys in the way so I couldn't get the door fully open, but I could see enough – Sarah wasn't in there.

The Minotaur door was open. I pushed it and the bottom dragged on the carpet but it kept moving until the wardrobe stopped it.

Downstairs there was some light-hearted commotion.

This room was huge. Master bedroom and an upstairs living room in one.

In front of one of the windows, between two floor standing speakers, there was a desk with a lamp and a half full pint glass of water. And it had two huge computer screens with an audio track on one, and a clip of a film with a woman in a wedding dress and blood all over her on the other.

I hit play, and the speakers boomed 'DON'T GO!' and I hit the spacebar to stop it, and the lamp rattled and I caught it before it came down.

Listened for the stairs, heard their laughs in a spin cycle.

On the other side of the bed there was another book case – one full of books I'd never seen before. And on the shelf in front of them the incense stick smoked. I spat it out.

In the hallway the frames on the wall teased me, shifted and reshaped, and one by one I pulled them down from their hooks, stuffed them under my arm. Didn't know who these people were, and I didn't know how they'd got our pictures or how they'd managed to recreate these scenes from our lives, but they couldn't keep them.

Now there were pictures of the boy and girl at school, with their dead green eyes and their green jumpers with their hair parted down the middle and tied in pigtails. I took them too, couldn't say why.

Felt myself starting to drown, gasping, like there was no oxygen, and my legs were going away from me and when I reached for the bannister I missed it or it wasn't there.

Leaned against the wall, split my weight on the outside of the stairs like before, and halfway down I looked through the balusters into the living room for Sarah's boot, but it was gone, and there in its place was the boy.

A little older than in the photos I had, maybe five or six now, but with the same dead green eyes that looked at me in the kind of stupefied way I was coming to expect. He was holding a folded over piece of burned toast, and there was red jam on both of his cheeks.

I could hear the parents talking. They were on the other side of the kitchen, which was huge if it was as big as all the other rooms.

I put my finger on my lip.

'Hello,' he said, still chewing.

He was about knee height. Putting him out of service would take no time at all and less effort, but the tiniest squeal from piggy and I'd be up against the Minotaur and whatever weapon he brought with him.

I whispered 'Hello.'

He whispered too, said 'Are you a monster?'

I thought about it. There was a mirror across from me, above the shoe rack. I didn't look.

'No. I'm the hero.'

'Are you looking for the monster?'

'Yes. Go and hide!'

He thought twice. Then he took his jammy and ran back to the kitchen.

I heard his dad greet him, and I knew I wasn't safe for long.

I had to move.

I dropped Queenie back in more or less the same place she came from, hugged the frames to my chest, turned the big gold knob in the centre of the door and didn't look back.

15. The Signpost

For a while I stood in a bus shelter out of the rain, thought about catching one through the windshield.

I didn't look at the pictures – stacked them against the bike and bumped my head gently against the perspex until the quakes stopped.

I tried to look on my phone at how big Warrester was, watched the time tick over to three p.m., and considered going back to ask the family I'd burgled if they knew who had the other F-Type, maybe get a jammy off them too.

I'd picked up the frames, and I was in the saddle, when just like Thatcher said, I heard the V8.

Just a hum in the wind. Getting louder, throatier.

Pinned the frames against the handlebars, chased it uphill, towards the roundabout. And I was flying, closing in, and at the top of the hill it hit the circle way too fast, a real piece of work, like an emerald bullet.

Looked out of control but the balance kept it straight, and it smoked back the way I came, and I span after it hard, fast, nowhere near fast enough. It burned away, and I followed the sound until the sound cut out.

Stalked the bypass. Down as far as the cricket club and back, and I was checking off the roads that splintered off when the hum came again, fired into the junction of a cul-de-sac called Bank View, thirty yards in front of me, and I hit the brake, buckled to a stop, and so did he.

In the blackout glass I saw myself panting, and I wanted to move, get the bike in front of him, but something made me hesitate.

Lifted a leg off, heavy with acid. Moved slowly, like catching a moth, bent to put the frames on the ground, and BOOM, he was gone.

No chance to chase this time. Uphill, nothing left in me.

By the time I had my phone out, the number plate was a yellow line.

Squatted down, picked at the lump and caught my breath. Two options occurred:

Option One, the kidnapper had Sarah tied and gagged next to him in that car. He and Daddy Salt had brought forwards their plans for whatever reason, and they were off to some sort of rendezvous and I was too late to free Sarah before she thought her family saved her from their own kidnapping scheme. She'd spend the rest of her life in her dad's pocket and I'd spend mine regretting not having thrown myself in front of the Jag when I had the chance. *If* I had the chance? Happened about thirty seconds before but already I had all the dimensions screwed up in my memory.

Option Two, Sarah wasn't in the car. The kidnapper had gone to check she was still cuffed to the radiator, and now he'd gone to buy a new butcher's knife. I had a window to get her out before he came back to cut her fingers off.

Option One was a dead end. Drive the car off a bridge.

I had to believe in Option Two.

Bank View was a cul-de-sac of twenty houses, and only one had an empty driveway.

Quasimodo-humped old bag said 'Cheer up, Clive,' to a man dragging a dead dachshund on a choke chain.

I looked over my shoulder, listened for the Jag, locked Liv to a garden gate whose claim to be in constant use would have been more convincing if a few generations of spiders hadn't webbed a blanket around it. Watched them go to work on a wasp, and I wanted him to get out, and he rolled and rolled himself deeper.

Amongst the five-star B&Bs and more turrets, number six was a bungalow made out of cheap sandy bricks, slotted into a space that wasn't meant for a house. The windows were cut into the walls with a Stanley knife and the white paint on the sills had run all the way to the drive.

The drive wasn't really a drive. Just a cracked up stretch of badly mixed concrete, with a mess of nettles and stingers and foxgloves tied around the border. They grew up a wooden archway halfway along the path to the front door, and nailed to the top of the archway there was a sign that said *Beware Dog*, and I didn't buy that one either.

Done with sneaking around, I pressed the buzzer.

Half expected Sarah to come to the door, ask me in for coffee.

Pressed it again, jammed my finger into it and listened for the buzz. Nothing. Little light came on for a second to take the piss. Doorbells didn't work. You know they don't work, and you still let them make a cunt of you.

Old Mondeo slowed down behind me, crept past. I watched it go.

Rapped my knuckles on the door. Still nothing.

Option One lingered, tried to catch my eye. I didn't look.

Lap of the house. Real step down from the last two properties but we were getting closer to my price range.

'You'll just adore this unassuming retreat for kidnapper and kidnapee, with a host of sturdy radiators and easy-wipe wood floors.'

Curtains all closed again. I stayed in the back garden, marked by an army of fir trees so the towers around it couldn't see in.

On the ledge inside the kitchen window there were a set of keys on a piece of string.

I put the frames down, picked up a baseball brick from a six-foot pile of rubble, and pitched it at the glass about as hard as I could.

'Don't let appearances fool you – this suburban fortress is fitted with reinforced glass windows to keep the neighbours' noses well and truly out of your abductions.'

I thought again. Threw a few more bricks at different windows.

Then I stepped back.

Cut like crosshairs through the middle of the skylight, this intersection of two cracks implied a different type of glass up there. Kind of glass you can put a brick through.

No ladder. Drainpipe another flimsy piece of shit.

Another lap, came back dragging a compost bin with a

missing lid, pushed it as flush as it went to the kitchen window.

Inside the bin there was a needle sharp set of hedge shears. I climbed in there with them, thought about throwing them out and by some divine twist of fate decided against it.

Put the brick in the last pocket that didn't have mulch or a phone or photos in it. Clamped my hands onto the rim of the bin, and in this rare synergy between the way I imagined doing something and the way it happened, I pulled my knees into my chest and sprung my feet up alongside them.

Held there on all fours like Spiderman or a new giraffe, looking at the shears between my legs and begging the bin to stop shuddering. When it did, I straightened my legs, balanced against the brickwork.

Now the gutter. The gutter and me. It felt a little like if it came down the whole back of the house would come with it. There was blood on one of my thumbs. I reached up and put my fingers in the halfpipe, and water and fir needles and maybe dead rats spilled out into my face and my hair, but then it didn't turn any more – stapled well enough at two brackets just outside of where I held it.

Tightened my grip. Pulled up slowly, always watching the brackets, seeing they didn't move. Got my left foot up against the brick above the window, and I reached with my right hand for a gap in the slate, and it felt strong.

The first time I kissed her she'd been crying, and I hated it when she cried. I think we'd been drinking, or at least I definitely had. She was sad because her old girlfriend was in a new relationship. Because of their history, she'd told Sarah they couldn't be friends anymore. Hadn't seemed much like friends to me anyway.

Her face was red, and her hair was a tangled mess. I wanted her to feel better.

When I kissed her, she pushed me away. We laughed about that later. She said she didn't know how to react, which made sense. Neither did I.

I pulled myself onto the slates, and when I started to slip backwards I steadied myself with a foot in the gutter, and I heard one of the brackets snap. By then it had done its job.

The front of my clothes were smeared in the green paste that iced the roof.

I crawled to the skylight and wiped a hole in the film of dirt, tried to look through but it was too dark to see anything except floorboards in the light below the window.

Ran my fingers across the crack, pushed against it and listened to the creak.

Took out the brick, swung once and the glass bowed inwards. On the second swing the whole skylight fell through, split apart on the boards like a sheet of ice.

'Now if you're concerned your victims won't have room to stretch their legs, we think this spacious loft conversion would make the perfect lair, complete with ensuite toilet and bedding facilities.'

I didn't need to dip my head in to get a load of the rancid smell. Did anyway.

Couldn't see all the way to the corners, around the disconnected toilet and a wooden high chair and a stack of damp boxes. Trap in the floor led maybe down to the front hallway, and it was open, half covered by a dirty mattress and a fort made of sandbag pillows.

And there was somebody there.

'This does come in at the very top end of your budget, but we've spoken to the bank, and they're prepared to consider you for their government-backed Buy to Kidnap scheme, which involves a fifty-fifty split of ransom payments over a fifteen year period.'

'Sarah,' I whispered.

Could hear her breathing, somewhere behind the pillow fort. Slow, short breaths.

I remembered what Gigger said about how traumatic it all would have been for her, so even with the kidnapper on his way back, I knew I had to be soft. Couldn't be associated with the fear of what they'd done.

'It's me.'

Leant in further, tried to get an angle to see her.

'Sarah…'

Felt a little like I was talking to a different person. Or like I was a different person. Both.

Heard the breathing stop. Knew she was listening. And I knew I only had one chance for a second first impression.

Kept my voice low, calm.

'I met this couple. Like a hundred years old.'

She shifted. Maybe turned over to face me.

'They've got this baggy neck, and they talk the same and they know a ridiculous amount about sports cars.'

Mattress creaked, and she sat up, and for the first time in months I felt her company, and when I cupped a hand over my eyes I could see her silhouette above the wall of pillows, and the gravity dialled up in me, and I wanted to get in there.

I said 'I feel a bit sick. Most of the time.' Whispered now. 'And I don't know if everybody feels like that. Or if to…I don't know…make myself sick or something.

Metaphorically.'

Not the reassuring pep talk I'd anticipated.

Said 'I've got this balloon inside me. Inflating.'

She was breathing faster again now, crying.

'And I never told you. And I should have told you.'

What was I talking about?

I was trying to work out if I could lower myself in head first, and I heard another shift in the mattress, and I started to feel like something was wrong.

Stayed where I was – half in, half out.

'Sarah.'

Crying louder, whining.

'What have they done to you?'

Her feet scrambled for grip against the mattress and the floorboards. The fort came down, and her trail leg sprayed white paper across the floor from a stack of folders. Brown eyes. Red around the edges. Teeth like new pencils. Huge. Monstrously big. And the snarl on her face shimmered with the sauce she'd marinate me in.

She hit the high chair and it crumbled under her, but she sprang off the seat anyway, came flying at the skylight. And the part of your mind that dares you to jump on the motorway held me there, and the part of it that keeps you alive pulled me out.

I got my head out of the hole, and when I did she came through it all in one go so I heard the border of glass tear along the length of her body. I rolled sideways and she swivelled to look at me, and her claws tried to dig in but my torso had made a greasy slide along the slate.

When she hit the gutter the second staple snapped like a gunshot, and when she hit the bin I heard the air rush out of her. The tips of the hedge shears came all the way through the back of her head.

I wondered what heart attacks felt like if they didn't feel like this. Lay on my back for maybe a minute in this meditative state, trying to repress having poured my heart out to a rottweiler.

Then I got up, dropped through the skylight.

No light switch. I crawled past the papers on the floor, squinted to see what was written on them but couldn't. Kicked a couple of boxes.

'Sarah?' I said again, but she wasn't there so she couldn't hear.

Shifted the mattress, looked down from the trapdoor to what turned out to be the living room, and with every rung I took of the ladder Option Two receded and Option One solidified.

Across the floor there were torn open bags of dried dog food, all empty, licked clean. Unopened tins too, some with teeth marks, thrown around and lined up in odd places. Shit everywhere. Whatever the dog had planned for me, I pitied her now. The shears were better than this.

No photographs, no mirrors, no clocks.

Spiders had found another way into the kitchen, and they'd seized the corner where the fridge should be and died waiting for a meal.

The dog's tail pointed like an antenna out of the bin. I opened the window to let some air in, closed it again when the tail twitched or went limp or blew over in the wind.

In the hallway by the front door, there was a nest of flyers for budget food stores and payday loans, cheap booze and credit cards. I kicked the nest, and a package rolled out.

It said *R.J.S., 6 Bank View, Warrester*, on brown parcel paper, screwed around a little box. Unscrewed it. On a piece of card inside, it said *Dear Robert. My Grandmother's ring, as promised. Roger Salt.*

The ring, like Sarah, was already gone.

16. The Last Supper

I dreamed we were walking through Hyphorn golf course, by Pound Road. We used to go there so Sarah could follow people's dogs and weigh up which ones she'd have me steal.

We were the only ones around, standing at the top of the ninth tee holding hands. The sky looked white, like a paper backdrop on a TV set.

Then the perspective somehow shifted so I was watching us from a few hundred yards away, maybe down by the hole, but I could still hear the conversation okay.

'It's cold,' Sarah said.

I took off my jacket and put it around her shoulders. For me it was quite warm, but that was usually how it went. I felt like I wanted to see her eyes, but I didn't try to look at her and she didn't look at me.

'This is the last time,' she said.

'The last time for what?' I asked her.

Somebody knocking the window woke me up. Had the feeling they'd been knocking for a while. My legs were numb and my ribs ached.

The knock came again, and this time I saw knuckles against the fogged up glass. I tried to open the door and realised that it didn't open on this side anymore, so I wound the window down.

'Helloo.' I wondered if it was the Police. Realised they might still be looking for Syn.

She was holding a metal flask that had steam coming from it.

'I saw the bike. Cheers.' She passed the flask through the window. I tried to remember her name but I wasn't sure she'd told me. Took the flask.

She had on a grey hood, and her hair came out of it at the sides.

'It's the soup of the day. I thought you might want something?'

'What time is it?' I asked, sounded like I was sleep talking.

'Half ten.'

'Half ten?'

I went to drink it and she warned me it was too hot, and she was right but by then I'd burned my mouth already so I carried on. Pretty flavourless, which suited me.

I knew I should thank her but I didn't want to speak. Tried to clear my throat without making too loud a sound. For a second she was gone, and then the door on the passenger side clicked open and she got in and closed it.

We sat for what seemed like a long time, not saying anything. I scolded myself on some more soup, got leek stuck between my front teeth and got it out again.

I felt her tense a little when she said 'You don't mind me being here do you?' but I gave her the best smile I had and it was okay again. 'I've—' she started, then stopped.

She rubbed a hole in the condensation on the windscreen. Sky was clear of clouds, but there wasn't a moon or stars either.

'I've got a friend who works at a restaurant on the river. La Marea.' She waited, but I didn't say anything. I didn't know what to say. She waved her hands around in odd patterns that didn't match up with what she was talking about. 'I used to work there before they got rid of the bar upstairs. Paid more than this place.'

I'd finished the soup. It seemed like a lot until I'd made the bottom of it, but now I realised how hungry I really was, and I got a little hopeful I knew what she was going to say next.

'It's half off for friends and family on Wednesdays between ten and eleven, so I thought, if I'm gonna eat there anyway, doesn't... Well I don't mind paying for you. If you wanted to'

She took her hood down.

I thought about it. I didn't know what she wanted from me, but I wanted two bottles of pinot grigio, and little Sainsbury's did it a lot cheaper than La Marea would.

The hole in the condensation was growing because I'd left the window open. I wound it up, took my wallet out of my pocket. Inside it there were a couple of lucky dips, two fivers, and a few coins. I showed it to her.

'I can pay,' she said. 'Really.'

I looked over at her and she pretended not to notice. The bruised ribs were far worse than the head injuries. If she wanted to buy me some wine to make it feel better then why would I turn her down?

I cleared my throat at the same time as I started the engine.

We went straight over at the roundabout, and I remembered that the flowers were still in my pockets, and a hollow feeling swelled up. I was thinking about Lucy, if I could go back to her and start again tomorrow. Go to Switzerland even. Go after Salt.

For now I concentrated on the road, because I didn't want to hurt the woman.

'My name's Amber,' she said.

I nodded.

'And you're Marco.'

I nodded.

She took out her cigarette case. It was a metal thing with a pattern around the outside, and a strip to strike matches on in the middle. She offered me one and I took it, and she lit it for me and one for herself.

'If you don't want to talk we don't have to.'

I didn't.

I wondered if she thought I was homeless, and this was some sort of outreach. If I missed another rent payment she'd be right.

There weren't many people on the streets by the river. A pair of lesbians twirled each other across a pelican crossing, gave me the finger like I ran them too close.

When we made it to the restaurant strip, she told me to loop around to the car park at the back. I went the wrong way down a one way street and I felt her suck air through her teeth.

Reversed in between two spots and waited.

'Okay?' she asked.

'Yeah, this door hasn't been opening…'

'Ah,' she said, and gave me a thumbs up and got out of her side, and I was waiting to follow her out but she stopped in the way.

I heard her say something to herself, and I was sitting in the passenger seat when she looked back in at me.

'You didn't find it today?' she said.

'What?'

'That.'

She was pointing out in front of her and I followed the finger to the space between two empty ones, and I climbed out and she stepped out of the way. I'd given up trusting my eyes. I walked to it and put my hands on the bonnet, left prints in the soot, ran them all the way over the windscreen and the perfect curve of the roof to the boot. Circled it. All the way around, and the spare blood in me rushed to my face.

Then I ran.

Two women in blue aprons were talking outside their restaurants, waiting for electric shutters. I went into a tiny pub on the corner but there was only a kid sweeping tiles inside and he said they were closed. There were other places without shutters but all switched off and locked up, and then there was La Marea – a tall glass-fronted restaurant, propped up on thick old wooden beams and lit with five watt bulbs.

I went in.

'There's no smoking in here, sir.'

Hadn't realised I still had it in my mouth, spat it on the carpet and stepped through three men in white who went to stamp it out.

There were scattered empty tables with pages of menus stacked between condiments, ugly vinyl ceiling tiles that made it look like an office after hours. Against the walls on shelves there were unoccupied fish tanks and car boot sale ornaments.

I was vaguely aware that the white shirts had turned to me now, but they didn't tell me to stop.

On the bannister upstairs there was this thrumming orange light.

She looked like a poster from a French film my dad took me to see. Title slipped my mind. Her hair swirled down at the sides and drew a curve around one of her eyes. Had on a zig-zag red dress and lipstick, and black heels, which you didn't see her in much because they rubbed her feet and twisted her ankles.

The fireplace fizzed like cheap lemonade.

'Marco?' she said, as if she didn't believe it either.

And I remember I couldn't work out if she'd had tears in her eyes before she saw me, or if it was a trick of the light. And in that trick second she looked up and joy spread across her perfect face. And in that trick second the flames hid him from me.

Then a cold wind rushed through the door downstairs, and I was really seeing things.

Things like the diamond ring suspended in the air between us. Like the guy on one knee at the end of it who hadn't clocked I was there yet.

'Marco?' he said. And he turned to look, in an open collar pink shirt and chest hairs waxed into a triangle. His nose pointed down towards his whitened teeth and his gums withdrew the other way. He'd got this painfully false look of concern for when he talked to customers, and he had it on now.

Jim Stant. Of all the cunts in the world, Jim Stant.

She said 'What you doing here?' Words spilled into each other after a few glasses of wine.

He said he didn't want any trouble, but you could tell a part of him did.

On the table there were two plates, one with half a slice

of lemon tart, and one with chocolate cake and ice cream. That was Sarah's.

He said 'Look, Marc, mate...' but I didn't let him finish. All my life I let people talk to me like a kid because the guy with the cane said it was better to bend over than lash out.

It was hot. Like sweltering hot. And there was the dehydration and the hunger and concussion and I guess the wholesale emotional breakdown that had been distorting things up until now.

I took my jacket off, left it on the carpet. Picked up the cake and Stant got up off his knee and stepped in front of Sarah like some white knight.

Everyone was shouting except me. Nothing worth repeating.

I frisbeed the chocolate cake plate at his teeth, and he ducked out the way just in time, left a smear of fudge in the deep cut of scalp his hairline deserted.

And I followed it in, and Sarah tried to grab me but I shook her off.

He got his arms up like we were going to box, and they were thick – way out of proportion like they wouldn't share the gym membership with his legs.

I bypassed them, got him by the collar, and he got me by mine, and I drove him at the fire. Had this vague plan to set his chest hair alight, steal the ring, have a go at proposing myself.

Crowd didn't like it, and they were trying to get control without getting their hands dirty.

We went down and he rolled me over like he wanted to fuck me, and he thought he had me pinned but then I got the first good dig into his bottom rib, and his face went white and he softened for a second and I got on top.

I hit his head on the fireplace stone and it sounded like a tennis shot. That shocked him like it kicked in a survival instinct. He pulled out his arm and elbowed me in the jaw, which didn't really hurt but it caught me off guard, and he grabbed me by the armpit and I felt his nails dig into it, and that hurt like hell.

I tried to nut him and he got out of the way and made it fifteen all.

Now he was getting up on one hand and choking me out with the other, and I kicked at his legs to keep him down and I spat in his face and it bounced back to mine.

Sweat came out of his eyes, and the veins in his neck tried to burst, and I knew I looked the same. I got my thumbs into the soft part on the underside of his wrists and pushed them in, and he tried to pull out but I wouldn't let him. He brought his knee up into my stomach and gassed me, and when I crumpled he took his hands off my throat.

And I tried to get up and he got hold of my head, pinned it down on the stone looking up at the mantel. There was a heat-warped painting of a man laughing at his reflection in a butcher's shop window. I liked it.

Felt my ears start to cook, and I tried to shift out but he hit me in the cheek, and I felt everything wobble and freeze. But it came back. I slapped him on his, and he got a little stunned, and I got myself half up and my arm hit a brass bucket with a spade and a pitchfork in it. They blurred into one and split back apart.

Stant jumped to his feet, and he was calling me crazy, trying to get to the crowd. I picked up the pitchfork, and I stabbed him in his arse and he yelped like the dog he was, and I grabbed him by the belt and he came back down, and I gripped his hair with the fork in his face, and I was about to put him in the fire when a woman shouted 'Taser taser!' and I lost control.

It took three of them to pick me up, partly because I didn't want them to, partly because I was so out of it.

Amber was telling me to stop struggling, but I didn't know how, and I couldn't see where her voice was coming from.

They told everyone to get out of the way so we could get down the stairs, and when they moved I saw Sarah. She was against the bannister, and Stant was in front of her and she was pushing him away, and her face was blotchy and red. One of the officers nearly slipped on the loose carpet but the other two steadied her. And then I could only hear Sarah's voice, and it tortured me.

17. The Cell

They put me in a pastel green box. On the wall it said: *You will be charged for any damage done to this cell* in black stencilled letters. They took my shoelaces out of my shoes, and kept my jacket and all my things. And they asked me if I needed to be looked at by a medical professional.

Through the night I played it out a thousand times. Pinned to the floor with my hands around my throat, grabbed for the pitchfork and lunged at him through the dark, convulsed at the taser. Got back down and did it all again.

Sometimes it felt like a dream, and I thought I might wake up next to her, at midday on a Saturday, with the sun on the back of the curtains. Used to squeeze her legs to get them working. She said she had honey for blood.

Early in the morning a fat man with a moustache and a thick pair of glasses came around shouting and woke everybody up for no reason. I hadn't slept. They gave me the smallest cup of water they could find and told me they'd make food – boiled potato wedges and beans with two button mushrooms, served in a wet cardboard box. Eventually they took it away.

Maybe two hours later he opened the door again. With him there was an old man and a woman with a walking stick. The man had a clipboard. He said they wanted to ask some questions about my treatment here. I shut my eyes and the door closed and the light from the hallway went away. Then I slept for a while.

When I woke up I pressed the buzzer and a different man came to let me use the toilet, stood there while I took a shit in a metal tin. Down the hall somebody was screaming. I spat some blood into the toilet and went back.

Someone that had just started their shift asked me if I needed to call anyone – that a woman called Amber had left her number. I said no.

Later they had me speak to a lawyer and give a statement. I'd been arrested on suspicion of Actual Bodily Harm, and when they had all the evidence they'd charge me. I didn't have anything to say to them, so I didn't. They told me I wasn't to come back to Warrester before the trial, or be seen anywhere within 500 feet of Stant, and they gave me a restraining order that said so.

Trial date was March twenty-first at the magistrates.

They gave me my things back – my wallet and keys and phone and ring box and what was left of the flowers and the polaroid halves – and one of them told me how to get back to Syn at the restaurant. It was a mile away, but it was pretty much one straight road. She said to be careful, and not to go into the restaurant, and then she smiled at me and the foundation on her face cracked around her eyes. I screwed the polaroids into a bin.

When I got home I put the heating on even though I knew I couldn't afford it, and I made myself a glass of milk, and I went to bed.

For the next few weeks nothing happened.

I stayed in bed mostly, and I let my phone die, and I didn't answer the door, and I didn't get the post. I lived on baked beans and noodles and a five kilo bag of rice.

After a while I realised I didn't want to be able to see my reflection. I sellotaped Christmas wrapping paper to the mirror in my bedroom, and shattered the one on the bathroom with my forehead.

One time I had a bath. I made the water as hot as I could with some cleansing ritual in mind, threw a couple of kettles in too, but then I couldn't get into it so I had to add some cold and wait a while for it to cool down.

I scrubbed my arms with the flannel until they were burned red, and I picked at the soft skin around my big toenails until both of them were bleeding. Then I tried wanking but I couldn't get hard and I thought about cutting it off with scissors but I couldn't reach any from the bath and it wasn't a good enough idea to get out for.

Stubbed my surgically improved toe on a storage box that had been in the living room since the day I moved in, and when I threw it at the wall I found a pair of my dad's old glasses that I'd kept one time when he was throwing things away. Black plastic frames, almost round, and thick lenses – particularly the right one because that eye's weaker. I put them on. Couldn't see most things through them, and they gave me a headache after a while but I kept wearing them.

Another time I heard this 'Three Blind Mice' ice-cream van chime, watched him stop on the crescent and considered going to get one. It was the middle of January. I'd lost a significant amount of weight. I looked around for some change, thought maybe I could swap him for a tin of coconut milk, and I had the key in the door when I changed my mind. Knew everyone'd be watching. Wouldn't give them the satisfaction.

After a while of nobody coming, the ice cream guy took a ninety-nine into the cab and got out, and he crossed over to behind Syn and onto the pavement. I briefly thought he was going to bring it up to me – that he'd seen my curtains move – but he didn't.

He unbuttoned his jacket and bent down, and he shook the cone so the ice cream dropped out of it onto the floor, and then he went and got back into the van, and drove away singing the tune.

And one by one the cats came out – from the houses all around, from under cars, and from their front fence watch-posts. They looked at each other with suspicion. I wanted to get down there, where the action was, but I stayed in the window and let it play out.

The ginger stray went first. Came from twenty-four's hedge, crossed over the grass and tried to look like he licked it by accident, scattered up Redman's fence and sat there working out if he liked being able to feel his brain.

I drank my milk, UHT stock but still tasted like turning.

Drive-by opened the floodgates. First the tortoiseshell, who ran like a spastic, ploughed his face in and didn't stop to breathe. Then the black twins from downstairs. They hit it hard, took a couple of swipes at Ginger when he tried to get back involved.

It was half way gone when the flap at number twenty

rattled. Percy.

Tortoiseshell tripped across the road sideways, took a goodybag in his whiskers. Twins didn't stay much longer, dipped away under Mr Singh's Ram and watched it unfold.

Percy was the size of three cats strapped together because he loved chicken fat and Mrs Radcliffe couldn't have kids. He was a sandy colour, with an ironed flat face and a bell on his collar to stop him raiding bird nests.

Ginger was blind in one eye, mostly deaf in both ears. When he saw the other three leave he let his stomach do the thinking, moved in.

Over the road Mr Simpson was wheeling out his blue bin a day too late, oblivious.

Percy didn't like Ginger because he was homeless and Radcliffe sometimes gave him scraps. He strained to see what was going on, and he sniffed the air and gained pace. Broke into a trot.

By the time Ginger heard the bell the fight was over. Percy went for his face and Ginger squealed, he bowled into him and stripped some fur off his tail before he let him get away.

I couldn't hear Percy purring because the window was closed, but I felt like I could. I unlocked it and pushed it wider than I'd ever stretched the hinges before, and I threw my glass of milk out at the bastard, missed, and shattered Syn's back windscreen.

Radcliffe was in her front window. She had her hand over her mouth.

I shut the curtains.

Everything was tainted. I thought maybe I could start a bonfire – her owl teacup, her letters, band t-shirts she bought me, unfinished paintings she stuck to the walls.

Everything. But every time I tried, throwing them out was worse – made everything final.

One day I tore off a few of the reindeer in the mirror to cut my hair. Thought I'd start again. Always wanted it like Jack in *Titanic*, but I couldn't admit it to my barber.

I didn't do a good job. Didn't have any pictures to work from because I'd burned the DVDs and I didn't have the internet because the wankers never came to fix it.

I cut too deep into the right side of my fringe, realised it's more of a sweep. Tried evening it out and put down the scissors when it started looking like Paul Weller, decided I'd have to shave it all off but never got around to that either. Assumed Weller had a similar story.

Eventually there were knocks on the door, distant unfamiliar voices through the letter flap. I never answered, stayed under the duvet – the bills were coming in faster than I could shred them, and the bailiffs were next.

I heard people talking outside. Heard Radcliffe tell them about the milk. Always knew she'd be in league with them if it came to it – throw me to the wolves.

I thought about faking my death. Get out of paying these people anything else, get out of facing Stant in court, and break Sarah's heart at the same time.

18. The BT Broadband Repair Man

I hadn't talked to anybody but myself for months. Every day I felt worse, looked worse, smelled worse. The apartment was rotting from the inside out and I was going with it.

Must have been three months. I'd lost track. Got sick of the clocks trying to discipline me so I'd dismantled them all and flown the parts in card aeroplanes over the back garden. Reached the bike shed twice.

Something woke me up. Made me jump. Sounded like an animal at first – going *chhhk chhhk chhhk*.

Evens on it being real. Up from two-to-one on the cat thing.

I breathed quietly and listened for a while, and it came more frequently. *Chhhk chhhk chhhk*. Three times in quick succession, then maybe ten times slowly.

Pushed the duvet off, clamped it back down to keep the heat where it was. Eyes strained to adjust to the sepia light. Went to stand up where the floor wouldn't creak but I put my foot down on my dad's glasses and cracked them, and for a second I wondered how I'd be able to see.

Legs had lost some mass. Knees ached, and the skin on them sagged where I'd spent a month testing which one was most elastic. Inconclusive. I made it to the door and pulled the dressing gown on, listened for footsteps.

Chhhk.

Now I felt the draught on my ankles – the open window – and I remembered him. The Hammer Man.

So who the fuck was The Hammer Man? If there was no kidnapping and he wasn't a kidnapper or a kidnapper's henchman, who was he? Except a guy who broke into my apartment every few months to try to bash my head in.

Chhhk.

Or grind my head in, or whatever he had planned this time.

I stood there playing with my knee skin, trying to work out what the hell he wanted with me that had sent him so crazy, and I even laughed at maybe his girlfriend left him too.

How did he keep getting in? I wasn't taking visitors, kept the windows and the doors locked. I'd lined the chimney breast with razor blades on Christmas eve.

Chhhk.

Who the fuck was this guy?

I didn't want a fight this time. Wondered if I could just walk out and meet him – pull open the door, tell him I wasn't in a good place and stretch my arms out, let him do what he wanted like Kenobi and Vader. Embrace death. Disarm him and do myself in if he didn't have the balls.

When Mick was the boss, he used to hang on the office door. Whatever I was doing, he'd say 'Daydreaming again, McGann?'

I'd smile at him and tell him something senseless about an account we didn't run, and he'd do this thing where he bowed sideways and nodded like he already knew it, and then he'd leave me alone.

I used to daydream about lying the car broke down so I could take a morning off. Now, I daydreamed about letting my burglar euthanise me in the living room.

The thought passed and the noise came again – *chhhk chhhk*. Different now, or I was hearing it differently. Less like a weapon, more like somebody screwing something together with a ratchet wrench.

I looked in the mirror through the gap in the wrapping paper. I was ill. Thinner and paler than I'd seen myself before. After whatever happened here was over, I'd sort things out – find more wrapping paper and maybe cover the windows too so I never had to look at myself again.

I tied the dressing gown and pressed my ear against the door. There was something else going on in there. Paper rustling, and a plastic bag. And *chhhk chhhk chhhk*.

Toyed with the prospect of the agency breaking in to change the locks. It was the most reasonable explanation, and I somehow knew it wasn't true.

Other than them there was only one person with a key.

I got an eye down on the floor, watched the shadows flick around like a zoetrope.

What did she want?

…

Maybe some sort of reconciliation. Maybe she'd left him – remembered what a snivelling little worm he was, and come crawling back to me. Softly softly catchy monkey.

Chhhk chhhk.

And maybe I didn't want the monkey. Bit of a shock to

the system for the little traitor that she can't just drop people and leave them running around the country breaking into people's houses while she fucks the manager.

Pulled at the knee skin. Whether I'd ever take her back or not, she couldn't see me like this. I thought about barricading the door with the bed, or climbing out of the window and running away for a few hours – hiding under the canal bridge, maybe steal a Sainsbury's extra thick.

Her voice seeped through. A soft whisper, barely perceptible. And shushed out. Extinguished by something deeper, coarse. She was with a man. *He* was there. There to keep her safe, as if I'd ever hurt her. I hated him. Couldn't believe she'd bring him to my house.

Chhhk chhhk chhhk.

And what was he *doing* in there? What could he possibly be *doing* in my house?

I was mad. For the first time in a long time I had something inside me. A purpose: to finish killing Jim Stant.

There was a woodlouse walking the door bar like he owned the place. Maybe he did. I jabbed a finger at him but I couldn't fit it under the wood, and I tried to blow him off course but that somehow just got dust in my eye and I sneezed.

...

Chhhk chhhk.

'Marco is a seemingly clever boy who seems unable to apply himself for any prolonged period of time and is far too easily distracted. If he is ever to achieve his ambition of killing Jim Stant, he will need to learn to pay attention to the task at hand for upwards of thirty seconds.'

There was something about being able to kill someone if they're in your house. Always on the news, with these pensioners with shotguns. And they talked about reasonable force. Self defence. And if they went upstairs then anything goes.

Well he was upstairs – the whole place was upstairs. So maybe it had to be the bedroom. Made sense – if they're in the bedroom they're not there for the TV. If they're in the bedroom they're there for you. And then it's all self defence, and it's all reasonable force.

Had to lure him into the bedroom. Never been good at that.

Looked around for ideas.

I'd tell them he came at me. Sarah's word against mine, and they'd throw out that bitch's testimony as soon as they heard what she'd done.

I got up, picked up the glass of UHT from the bedside drawers and poured a little of it onto my hand and smoothed my hair to one side, then I drank what was left so I didn't make a mess when I slashed his neck.

Had a tricky idea, but I liked the look of it.

Stood with my back to the door, put the fingertips of my free hand against the knob and teased it around, and when the latch clicked open, I fixed the dressing gown onto the hook and hung the seven stone there was left of me from it. And like a bat, I waited.

Chhhk chhhk chhhk.

There was no-one to taser me now.

Chhhk chhhk.

No-one to stop me.

Chhhk.

'Rotten in here, man,' he said. 'Smells like you've shit the bed.'

On the settee there were two people. One an old woman with pink slippers, and the other, with a bag of chips in his lap and a spliff the size of a battered sausage hanging out of his mouth, her son, Tommy Gigger.

'Afternoon sunshine,' he said, and he smiled with the spliff between his teeth. He held up his hand and showed me his lighter, pushed his thumb down on the wheel. It went *chhhk*, but didn't give a flame. 'Haven't got a lighter in there have you? One you've not sniffed all the fluid out preferably.'

His hair was greyer in the winter, and it was longer than the last time we met. He said haircuts were a construct designed to distract and numb, although he'd always have a snip before a wedding. On the chest of his grey hoodie, he'd painted the word NEGLECT in block capitals.

His mom was snoring on every other intake of breath, and her eyes were flickering slightly. Whether she was actually asleep I wasn't sure. Seemed unlikely.

I went to the bedroom and came out with a pound shop pack of five lighters I hadn't opened, handed it to Gigger. He took one and lit up.

'Got you some chips,' he patted what was left of the two-seater and I sat down, put the milky-white glass I'd been holding at my feet. 'Clive Trout,' he said, and pulled my bag out from behind the old lady, who'd been keeping them warm. 'Only place still wraps in newspapers.' He swapped the spliff in his mouth for a chip with some transfer rumours on it. 'And you can taste the difference, man – you really can.'

I peeled back the entertainment pages. Gigger liked an aggressive amount of salt and vinegar. He handed me over the spliff and I hit it. For a while we just sat there and ate, and snored. He told me the window was staying open until he couldn't smell my breath, and I told him to get fucked.

In the corner of the room there was an open suitcase with a blow-up bed in it, and a rolled up sleeping bag and one of those big V-shaped pillows smothered in pink polka dots.

I didn't ask how they got in, or how he seemed to already know what happened. I knew the answer.

'I was gonna put a stew on,' he said, chewing, chewing, 'but the old bat said she'd get her purse out.' He looked over at her and wiped a line of dribble from the corner of her mouth with a tissue. 'Strapped to the underside of the commode, man.' Shook his head, posted in another chip.

Half a bag down my stomach started sending things back, and as well as he hid it I knew it unsettled Gigger seeing me like I was.

'Don't have to finish it in one go. Just pick at it.'

I wrapped up what was left and put it on the floor, and I leaned back in my seat and tried a deep breath. He balled up his newspaper, dropped it next to mine, and he put his arm on my shoulders.

When I woke up I felt awful, which was better than I'd felt in a while. The old woman was sitting reading a print-off of a newspaper from nineteen eighty-six with a magnifying glass. She had Gigger source them for her from the records at the city library.

I sat up and she looked over.

She raised her eyebrows to salute me and I tried saying good morning but my voice cracked it out of range.

'Tommy?' I asked. She turned back to the newspaper and thumbed towards the front door, and I took the opportunity to stand up on the half-deflated mattress and tuck my cock into my waistband.

She smelled of talcum powder and shandy. That meant it was after twelve.

The last time she'd spoken to me – to anyone other than her son, as far as I knew – was at her husband's funeral. Others she thanked for coming, but me she looked at in this serious way, with these ice blue eyes, and she said 'You'll look after Tommy.'

I could see the veins in her legs through her tights, and her kneecaps kept shifting around because she was constantly tapping her slippers on the laminate to keep the blood flowing. She'd seemed to age quickly for a while, but now she'd looked the same for a decade and everyone else – Tommy, my dad – we were catching up.

I picked my nose and scratched out a blackhead on the inside of a nostril, drank some water, tried to suppress the urge to piss until I could be sure I'd hit the target. Then I went into the bedroom to get changed. On the pillow there was an envelope with my name on it. The writing was a scrawled black mix of barely legible twists. As far as I could tell, it said:

Marco,

Shakespeare can cut the crap – I'll tell you now, it's better to have never loved at all. He'll have been the slag doing the dumping.

Fifteen years ago today, Asa's car got rammed off the Warrester Road Bridge by a lunatic who'd kidnapped a little girl.

I read it again.

Fifteen years ago today, Asa's car got rammed off the Warrester Road Bridge by a lunatic who'd kidnapped a little girl.

Maybe I knew it was Warrester once, or maybe it never came up. Or maybe I'd done some permanent damage now and everything would be crazy forever.

I thought about sitting in the tree by the doctor's surgery with Gigger on the day of the crash. We were going to see *Lost in Translation* at the Odeon because both of us loved Bill Murray. Don't think I ever saw it afterwards. We had cans of Tizer and we talked about his dad coaching our football team. And we laughed about him holding the windows closed and farting on the way to games.

I've spent fifteen years trying to sulk myself to death. It takes six pills in the morning to sit me up, and another six to get me to sleep at night after a bowl of whatever sewage Tommy's served up (bless his cotton socks).

By the looks of it, you could sulk yourself to death in a matter of weeks, so you're much better at it than me.

You look, frankly, as bad as I've ever seen a living man look. You're a bag of bones, and you've obviously gone a bit doolally tap,

Obviously.

so I thought it wouldn't hurt to tell you what I think of it all – it can hardly make things any worse.

When you were a little boy, you used to sit on my wall in my front garden, and you'd ask me for a choc-ice, and you'd tell me all about which teacher you'd told to fuck off that week.

You'd say with all sincerity that they'd started it, and they treated you like a fool, and they deserved exactly what they got.

They'd send you to your nana's, and your dad would go in and argue til he was blue in the face why they shouldn't exclude you. Then you'd come round for a choc-ice and tell me you'd done it all over again.

The thought of my dad made my spine hurt.

You were a little Jack-in-the-Box, and sometimes you were right, and most of the time you were wrong. Either way, once you popped out there was no winding your neck back in. They knew it, your dad knew it, and I knew it for sure.

When you grew up, you wound it in yourself so they'd give you a job. Polished your smile and put a bit of spit in your hair, and you looked lovely. Got yourself a house in the better end of town, and a nice posh girl who said she hated the same things you did.

Then one day, just like me, you found out it had all been a scam.

Now, the police, the courts, the posh girl, they might look at what you went and did next and say you lost your mind. They're wrong.

Going after what they've had off you, not taking any prisoners, holding people accountable, that's not losing your mind.

Losing your mind's sitting at home for fifteen years feeling sorry for yourself and doing nothing about it. What you're doing now, that's losing your mind.

If that's what you want to do, be my guest. Get in bed with me, and we'll have a whale of a time eating shit stew twice a day for the rest of our lives.

If not, I'd suggest you let the Jack back out the box.

Love,
Sylvia

P.S. Burn this in case it all goes tits up.

I peeled back a reindeer.

The old woman was clearly unhinged. Maybe off her meds. I'd had a couple myself and there was no doubt Gigger was at them too.

Then the key turned in the front door and it came open, and I listened to Gigger's boots make it up the stairs, tucked the letter away and followed them into the living room.

'Morning morning,' he said. Maybe it was just relative to myself, but I thought he looked damn healthy. Pink in the cheeks. He had a spliff wedged behind each ear and I supposed one of them was for me. He took off his rucksack and put it down at the foot of the mattress, then he looked at his mom, still trawling through business news, and said 'Nap?' She nodded, and he picked her up like she didn't weigh a thing and took her into my room, came back and handed me the bigger one. He lit them both and opened the window.

'How's it going, man?' he said.

'I'm okay,' I told him.

'Good, good.' He pulled the rucksack over and opened it, took out sweet potatoes and a white bloomer, and milk and red lentils, and then his original PlayStation and a couple of dual-shock controllers. 'Thought we'd have a game while the stew's on, man.'

'Yeah.'

He took the food into the kitchen and put the kettle on.

'Oh,' he called through, 'grab the right front pocket of the bag, man.' I dragged it over with my foot and unzipped it, and I pulled out two honeycomb choc-ices, both crushed a little out of shape. 'Mom said get us one each.'

Then I smiled for what felt like the first time, pissed myself.

He'd had the lentils soaking in a mixing bowl for a few hours when he went to peel the potatoes. I stayed in the living room and played *The Wrath of Cortex* until I got to a scuba-diving level, then I joined him. We'd had at least an eighth between us, and this was top-shelf stuff so I was spaced. Gigger looked fine.

I jumped up onto the sideboard above the washer-dryer and it made a cracking noise like it didn't want me there. Gigger had been whistling 'Love Will Tear Us Apart' through his teeth, but now he stopped.

He tucked his hair behind his ear and stirred two pans at the same time, took a drink from a funny looking tea.

'What level you on?' he said.

'Ah...I can't remember what it's called. The second underwater one?'

He bobbed his head like he still had Joy Division playing, and his hair dropped back over his ear, 'Deep Trouble, man.'

'Deep Trouble,' I agreed.

'Sharks everywhere.'

'Thought I'd watch the master at work instead.'

'Good to take a step back from it.'

He dipped a wooden spoon into some red sauce and tasted from it, wrestled the cap off a pepper mill I didn't know I had.

The black mould from the bathroom had moved into the kitchen, and there were mushrooms sprouting like spice racks above the window. Soon it'd be in the bedroom. But what could I do? When we moved in the landlord suggested opening the window a few times a day, didn't mention the broken extractor, didn't mention the water-based paint he'd used to cover it up in the first place. Really the only way out was to burn the whole thing down, but it was maybe too damp to catch alight.

'Sorry about the money,' I said.

Gigger turned around and looked at me like he wasn't sure I was talking to him. When it turned out I was, he put his spoon down on the side and leant back facing me.

He said 'We're all sorry about the money, man.'

'But you know—'

'I know you'd do the same for me.' He looked at me with his green and red eyes, and then he went back to the stew and lit a dog-end on one of the hobs. 'There's a bit more in your wallet, man. Fill the tank.'

And that was the end of the conversation.

When the stew was done we took a bowl each. Every once in a while Gigger went and checked on his mom, fed her, and took her the paper and her pills. He said she was too tired to want to come out again. We played *Crash*, took turns with deaths. And we smoked, and he showed me something new he'd been working on with the ukulele, and it was pretty scrappy but you just knew it was a hit.

The next day when I got up they were sitting together.

Her on an iPad and him playing one of the *Halo* series on an Xbox. He had on a headset, stalking somebody with a rocket launcher.

I went to the bedroom and put clean pants on from a stack of fresh clothes someone made, and I was halfway into a pair of jeans when I opened the door back to the living room.

'How are you on the internet?' I asked. They both stopped and looked up at me, and a thirteen-year-old American sniped Gigger's Master Chief and he ragequit.

The old lady went back to her tablet, zoomed in to single-word level.

'Funny that, man,' Gigger said, motioned over to the corner of the room, 'It was all there – just needed…slotting together.' I walked around the settee and looked at the socket and the router, glowing steady blue like it never went away. 'I just wired it up, you know.'

I couldn't work it out.

He said that was how they made money – a real racket, man.

19. The New Job

When the letter came through the door I was on the toilet. Had a little pink in my cheeks, completed *Crash* to a hundred and six per cent. On a roll.

Gigger knocked.

'It's about the court date,' he said. 'I thought you said it was months away?'

'Why, when does it say?'

'Says it's in two days, man. Saturday hearing to accommodate a key witness – be the lad Stant I 'spose.'

'Two days?'

'There's something else, McGann.'

'Go on.'

'It says the charge was upgraded to GBH. It'll be at Birmingham Crown Court in front of a judge.'

Gigger said not to think about the worst case scenario. The worst case scenario was fifteen years in prison, so I was thinking about the worst case scenario.

'What the fuck's he said I've done?'

'It says it'd have to be serious injury. And the worse one's if you *set out* to cause serious injury, which obviously isn't the case if you've just had a bit of a knock about and stabbed him on the outside of his trousers with a medium sized pitchfork.'

I could see him in the court, bandaged up, grinning with his gums at me in the dock.

'So you're saying there's no chance I'm going down for fifteen years?'

'I'm not saying there's no chance of anything, I'm saying we've got a day to get you a haircut, a suit, and a job interview.'

'What good's a fucking job gonna do if I'm in Strangeways?'

'Listen to what I'm saying, man.' He gestured for me to sit down, and I did, head in hands. 'These cases aren't about upholding the law, and they're definitely not about justice, or half the ruling class would have their heads on spikes across Tower Bridge. These are about whether you look, seem, act, like the kind of chap the people upstairs want to see walking around the Cornbow Centre on a Sunday morning. They want you looking sharp, kissing arse, and they want to see that you're participating in society as they think you should be.'

Knew he was right. Rubbed my fingers into my eyes.

My laptop screen was cracked and the crystals were starting to bleed into one another. Squeezed my thumb into the crack and blacked out another square inch.

Gigger was rolling a new one to help me through it.

I hated work. Hated getting out of bed, rushing showers, waiting in traffic to get somewhere I didn't want to be. Emails, phone calls, meetings, and unpaid lunch breaks.

More than anything, I hated the people. The hoops you had to jump through to die in your own bed were sickening.

Sending out creeping applications about how much you'd love to do it all for them was maybe the only thing worse. And they knew that, and they bashed you round the head six or seven times with the same question just to make you prove what a pathetic little bootlicker you are.

I'd been watching the cursor for a few minutes, hoping it had some ideas.

Gigger said 'Parcels?'

I said I didn't have a van.

He said 'You're not gonna need a van to get an interview.'

'It says do you have a van or suitable vehicle?'

'Say aye, I've got a van. All taxed and insured.'

Typed it in.

He said 'Doesn't matter if it says you need a fire engine, man. All we care about's can we get an interview in the calendar that's gonna make the bloke in the wig think you're not just a workshy little stoner.'

'Like you?'

'Aye, but they didn't catch me, did they cunty?'

He had a bong on his lap now – big green thing called Chernobyl, with an ice tray slot in the middle. Trying to set the gauze straight.

Felt behind my ear and found the spliff.

I sent off thirty applications per bong hit. Bottom of the barrel. Full time hours, fuck all pay. Scams, pyramid schemes, you name it. I called in, sweet talked, lied, lied, lied. Bled the sites dry.

Every shit job in the Black Country. Wrote cover sheets like I've always dreamed of being a grave digger, and you could eat your dinner off toilet bowls I scrubbed. Deleted them and sent some dreary desperate shit Gigger dictated.

Maybe hundreds, maybe thousands. Maybe like sixty and it just seems like more when you're reeling them off.

I was out of ideas, and we were playing this game where you try to make a mug spin around as many times as you can on the laminate, and Gigger had this elastic band operation going, and it was hard to tell through the smog, but either me or him was saying how the job market was a hall of mirrors, when the other one said 'Why don't you look for things like you used to do?'

I said 'Logistics? I couldn't stand doing that stuff again,' and Gigger rubbed his fingers in his eyes and I remembered that wasn't the plan.

Typed it in: Electronics logistics.

200 vacancies. I looked for shady adverts – kind of places might skim through the process, maybe buy a fake reference. Companies I knew cut corners or turned staff over fast.

The old lady was calling Gigger on his mobile but he was trying to engineer some downforce around the rim with some blue tac and a Farm Foods flyer. Let it ring out. Ringtone another ukulele anthem. Usually she wanted another drink or the channel changed because we were using the batteries for the TV remote in the second controller.

I was half watching him, half scrolling, scrolling, looking for a name I recognised, and a name I recognised turned up.

Grainy logo of a claret and blue truck, driven by a faceless man with his thumb out the window.

I used to say Stant would have killed for that guy's charisma. Stick photos of his face on the banners in the office.

Rhoder & Dalt Logistics.

Followed the link.

It said: *Junior Account Manager needed to join our fantastic team. 14,000.00–17,000.00 per year. Excellent benefits package. Under responsibilities it listed: Assist management of 4 customer accounts.*

Prompt analysis of customer queries. Ensure timely settling of customer invoices. Contribute to continuous improvement of procedures to improve efficiency of the purchase ledger and expense functions.

This was *my* job. The job they said they'd lose in the restructure – roll into another one to keep the company competitive. The job Jim Stant sacked me out of, made me lose Pound Road, made me lose Sarah. I looked for Gigger but he was in the bathroom or somewhere. It was *my* job. *My* job. Missing a chunk of money. And it was missing something else.

I went to the company website, checked the staff profiles.

Sharp, Hoffner, Shi – the Account Managers were all still there, grinning like they had guns on them. Their accounts orbited their decapitated heads – pharmacists, betting shops, garden centres. No.

Checked Jerry Matthews but they hadn't even promoted him yet so there was no way he'd be trusted with what I was looking for.

Googled it. Three links. Page not found. Page not found. Page does not exist.

I couldn't think straight. There were cats fighting outside and I didn't even want to watch them.

Span through it all again. Combed newsletters from the last six months. Nothing. A black hole – there was no mention anywhere of the biggest account at the company. My fifth account. The Post Office had disappeared from the face of the Earth.

No way they could have lost the account. No way. Without the Post Office I didn't see how Rhoder & Dalt could survive, let alone hire somebody new.

Gigger was back and he had a new spliff in his mouth, and he was firing a turret on the back of a Warthog with deadly accuracy.

I was excited.

I got up and put the kettle on and ate some bran flakes and made everybody tea, changed over to *Storage Hunters* which turned out not to start for another forty minutes.

Gigger said he thought it was strange too, scanned a couple of industry blogs he tracked, looked through Twitter. Nobody gloating about the Post Office changing supplier. Nothing.

Under Stant's profile it said in all caps:

FOR ENQUIRIES REGARDING UNATTACHED ACCOUNTS, PLEASE CALL ME DIRECTLY VIA YOUR CONTACT SHEETS.

I said 'Stinks of a coverup.'

'A coverup?'

'The Post Office isn't some unattached account. It's the crown jewel of the company. Like fifty per cent of the revenue. It's a cash cow.'

He looked hesitant.

I said 'Stant's done something.'

He said 'Like what, man?'

'He's deleted everything about the biggest account at the company from the website... He's hiding something.'

'Hiding what?'

I didn't have the answer and he knew I didn't. I was smearing some Mr Sheen across the front of my work boots with an index finger.

He said 'And what good's it gonna do you going breaking a restraining order two days before a Crown Court hearing trying to find out?'

I didn't look him in the eyes.

'It's not about Sarah.'

'I never said it was about her, man.'

'The Post Office has vanished off the face of the Earth.'

'The Post Office has vanished off the face of the Earth.'

'You can make anything sound ridiculous repeating it.'

'I'm not trying to make it sound ridiculous. If it sounds ridiculous, it's because it sounds ridiculous.'

'I've done the applications. What if nothing comes back? Or what if it does and Stant's got some crazy story worked out and the judge doesn't give a fuck how many job interviews I've got?'

He put the controller down. Sharpened the creases on the rim of the mug.

I said 'He's got me. Hook, line, and sinker. He's gonna have some expensive lawyer, he's gonna have Sarah sitting there saying I've got a history of violence. They're gonna throw everything I've ever done at me.'

Tapped the backs of his fingernails against the handle, looked up at me, and it rang out like a school bell. Said 'What, and you think if you can get something on him, he might drop the charge…'

'If he's lost the Post Office or something, and the directors don't know about it… I don't know. I don't know what he's done. It's intuition. Call me directly via your contact sheets? You think Mick would have done something like that? He'd have had kittens. Something's going on.'

I looked for his approval, didn't blink, and he pulled back this elastic belt he'd wrapped around the belly of the mug, and he held it there tight, and when he let it go it whipped into a spiral, and we watched it for what seemed like a lifetime, and it gripped the corners of the room and screwed them with it, and the colours bubbled into each other and drained into grey. When it slowed down things rewound, and colours loaded back up, and the corners more or less reset.

The mug shuddered to a stop, and Gigger watched it all the way.

'I bet he's embezzling,' he said.

'Embezzling?'

'Biggest crime in the world, man. Everyone's at it. Remember Mr Hill?'

'What, the Caretaker?'

'Remember he had that house built next to school?'

'The thing with no windows?'

'All over the *Chronicle* – never paid a penny for it. Borrowed the mortgage against the school, paid it off out the estates budget over sixteen years. They thought he had an assistant on twelve grand a year.'

'Yeah, Boomer?'

'Turned out Boomer was his son. Got him in every few weeks to make it look legit, man.'

'You're kidding? What, and he slipped up?'

'Gets madder and madder. Hill's wife says she wants a new conservatory put on the back or she's gonna leave him, so he tries to tell the Head he needs a new Executive Cleaner. Head says there's no space in the budget, and if anything he needs to cut Boomer's hours because nobody knows what he does around the place. Hill's obviously shit his pants he's gonna lose the lot, lost the plot and started putting sleeping tablets in the school dinners during GCSE season.'

'...'

'He's thinking if they sleep through the exams, fail the lot, the Head gets sacked and he keeps Boomer and sneaks the wife in as Executive Cleaner while the place changes hands.'

'That's fucking mental.'

'Gets worse. Top brass dinner lady walks in on Hill powdering the lasagne, runs and tells the Head, and the Head says they'll deal with it internally – not to get the police involved. She can't believe her ears, but the Head tells her he'll give her a two grand bonus if she keeps her mouth shut. Hill goes out on gardening leave for the rest of the exams, and the dinner lady goes off on holiday to Marrakech.'

'One of them talked?'

'No secrets in the workplace, man, as you well know. Soon as the dinner lady hits the tarmac, the rest of the team goes knocking on the Head's door asking for a piece of the pie. Cuts a deal with them and gets them all signing a non-disclosure agreement that's not worth the paper it's written on. Meanwhile, Hill's wife's told him he's got two weeks to finance the conservatory or she's out the door, and she's taking him for everything he's got. Poor bastard's totally off his head now – he's riding around in a Deliveroo outfit, holding up pizza shops with a BB gun.'

'He's like seventy?'

'Seventy-six. He's got eight grand in takeaway boxes when they sting him in Domino's on the Clement Road in town. Five armed police in aprons and baseball caps.'

'You're fucking joking.'

'I'll bring the paper tomorrow. By the time they get him to spill the beans, the whole PE department's on an all-expenses-paid golf trip to the Algarve, French and Spanish have got a box at the Nou Camp for the last day of the season, and English have got enough copies of *Lord of the Flies* for one between two as long as no-one forgets to bring it in.'

'You're taking the piss.'

'Aye, about the last one, but it's not far off how pathetic some of what they asked for was. Anyway, it turns out the reason the Head was so keen to cover it all up had nothing to do with reputation or anything like that. He had a background in accountancy, knew exactly what Hill was doing soon as he took over, liked the sound of it himself. He'd had two imaginary personal assistants on the books for five years, getting twenty grand each. They had a little office next to his, phone numbers, fancy email signatures. Entered them in the Secret Santa, even gave one of them employee of the month.'

'Fuck off...'

'On Mom's life.'

'So, what, are they closing it down?'

'Exam results came back better than last year. Passed the emergency Ofsted. Governors still liked him more than the last few heads and they didn't want to rock the boat. Voted unanimously to keep him and all the staff, including the PAs, rent out the school as a paintball centre over the summer to pay off the debt, and forget it ever happened.'

'You've made this up.'

'Ask anyone, man. I'll bring the papers in – they've been running the story for a month. Every one of them got away with it.'

'Even Hill?'

'Well, no – Hill went away for ten to fifteen for drugging the kids, but they didn't do him on the mortgage because the school didn't press any charges.'

'I don't believe you.'

'I wouldn't either. The point is: everyone's at it.'

I'd always wanted to play paintball at the school. Knew Gigger did too. Gave it maybe a sixty percent chance any of what he'd just told me was true.

I said 'Everyone's at what?'

'Embezzlement, man. Everyone's got their hand in the till.'

'What, so you think Stant's doing the same?'

'Formula applies across the board: long as you keep the

shareholders' bowls full, nobody's checking what you do with the rest of the stew. Who wouldn't give themself a bit more, man?'

'How dyou prove it?'

He picked up the bong, looked through the ice and his face distorted around it. 'Haven't got the foggiest, man. Depends what it is he's doing, if indeed he's doing anything at all.'

'Which he is.'

'So we think.'

He flicked his lighter open. *Chhhk*. Flame burst out, and he hovered it around the nugget of weed stuffed in the pipe.

'If you get caught, you're gonna make things worse for yourself,' he said.

'I won't get caught.'

He smirked because we both knew that wasn't true.

'I'll keep an eye on your emails,' he said, and I put my hands on his shoulders and kissed him on the forehead, and some of the tar from my lips smudged over.

20. The Quiff and The Razorblade

When I got into the centre of town the clock tower by Wilkinson's said it was ten-past one. That had been six minutes slow since the Two Thousand New Year, when someone cut the fuses on all the fireworks and they had to delay the Millennium.

I drove into the multi-storey. They'd coned off the disabled spaces at the front now, and if there hadn't been a guy repainting the wheelchair symbols I'd have had one anyway, but I didn't want to squabble. Eventually I beat a twelve-year-old reversing in on the top floor, and I sat in the car and thought for a few minutes while he tried to manoeuvre away without shunting the end I'd left sticking out.

It wasn't about Sarah, but it kind of was. Good to be honest about that, yeah.

I lit a cigarette. Treated myself to a pack of straights. Smoked in the vanity mirror and had a go at blowing rings.

Stant had us both in a vice. He could put me away for fifteen years, waste whatever youth I had left, ruin any financial prospects, sure. The ring on Sarah's finger was a life sentence.

Just like he did when Tompkins left Rhoder & Dalt, with Sarah, Stant had waited in the wings, bided his time, and when he saw weakness, he'd pounced. He was an opportunist. A poacher. And he'd poached Sarah, and he thought he had me caught in a trap.

First step was get myself free.

Gigger said embezzlement went from little fines to ten years depending how hard you bribed the judge. That was obviously worth something, but I knew Stant, and I knew the satin shirts and the fifty-six pound haircuts. His reputation – as a shit-eating sycophant who'd risen to the top despite none of the odds being stacked against him – meant everything.

If I was going to scare him away from taking me down in court, threatening his reputation was the key. I'd find something concrete, reveal whatever scam he had going on the Post Office, and I'd wave it under his nose, and I'd tell him if he didn't call off the trial I'd send it to the board or publicly humiliate him or whatever.

First, I needed to get into his office. Easy.

After last time's abrupt dismissal I guessed security wouldn't be so lax. They might even be on the look-out specifically for me, and if they got a hold of me I'd breached the restraining order and the GBH sentence was getting multiplied. It was high-stakes stuff, so a smash-and-grab wasn't worth the risk.

The fire escape was an option if I could be sure it wouldn't trigger the alarm. But how could I be sure?

I decided the measured thing was to walk around the

perimeter — scope the building out a little — try to get inspired.

That turned out bad for morale — the place had always been well guarded, but Stant's paranoia and the new ownership had obviously led to considerable upgrades, so now it had cameras to spy on other cameras, and they'd put in new sealed windows so nobody could get in or out.

Through the main glass doors my pal Tuppence was playing noughts and crosses with himself at the front desk. Always looked like he was trying to work out what the smell was on his top lip, and I had a feeling I knew.

I moved out of the way, back towards the fire escape. Standing there scratching myself, reconsidering the smash-and-grab, when the perfume of burned cheese drifted out of Patterson and Son's Café, followed by what I thought was my reflection in the front door until the door closed and left it there.

I was trying to read his name badge but my eyes didn't see detail well since wearing Dad's glasses, and maybe some of the lettering was worn away where he'd nervously fiddled at it like he was now.

Whatever his name was, he was the man at Sarah's desk — who'd taken her place — still wearing the same purple jumper, still the same sandy quiff, still irrefutably the double of me.

In his walk there was this boyish elasticity that underlined him being maybe five years my junior, and he thought he could use it to swerve me but I wasn't going to leave enough pavement for that.

I stuck out my hand.

'Marco McGann,' I said. He was wary, acting the kind of relaxed you do when you think it makes you less likely to get stabbed. He shook with a wet palm and cold fingers.

'You remember me…Rick?'

I could tell he did.

'Erm, yeah,' he said. 'The drawers.'

'That's right, the drawers,' I smiled, squinting a little to make myself look professional and thoughtful and to hide how red my eyes were. 'Look Rick—'

'Nick.'

'Nick. Look, Nick, I need to get into the building.' I watched his fingers twitch up towards the lanyard around his neck, then think better of it. Thought for a second I might have to beat the living shit out of him to get my hands on it. The fight in my head was a freakshow because of how disturbingly similar we looked – the disappointing bone structure, the crooked nose, the disinterested look he couldn't moisturise out of the bags under his eyes.

He glanced nervously at a cluster of cameras above us, said 'We were told not to talk to former employees.'

'They said that?'

'They emailed us a few months ago.'

'Really?' I said. 'Suspicious, isn't it? You've got to ask yourself why not? Huh?'

'Something to do with poaching.'

'Poaching?!'

'Like scouting…'

'Come off it. They're hiding things – the management.'

'Hiding th—'

'I bet you can all feel it? Rumours flying. What are they hiding?' He thought I was crazy, and maybe I did too but I had to find out for sure. 'Remember how they threw me out before? A respected former staff member? Makes you think, doesn't it?'

'I mean, I suppose so,' he said, warming to me.

I put my hand on his shoulder for what was supposed to

be a pat but maybe lingered into something less appropriate. Solid – he'd done better out of our shared genetics than I'd hoped.

'Listen, I don't wanna bore you so I'm just going to put my cards on the table.'

'Okay?'

'Those bastards are up to something in there and I need to get into Stant's office to find out what it is or I'm going to the clink.' He was a sceptic – I could see him trying to hide it, looking for a way out. There wasn't one. I said 'You ever noticed how much we look alike?'

'You and him?'

'Me and you.'

'Erm—'

'You have – you must have.'

He was looking at my hair and the bristles on my chin, so I told him I didn't mean the hairstyle and I knew I needed a shave.

'Look, how much do they pay you? Seven-fifty?'

'Eight ninety-one.'

'Bastards. No holiday?'

'Agency.'

'Bastards.' I took out my wallet. 'I'll give you ten for thirty minutes.'

'Thirty minutes of what?'

'You on lunch?' I asked him.

He nodded.

'How long you got left?'

Looked at his watch. 'About twelve minutes.'

'Perfect.' I took him by the arm and we jogged to Boots.

I explained to him when we got there that the tenner included the cost of materials – the shaving cream and the razors and the weird putty he said was how he got his quiff like that. Take-home was more like a fiver, but that was still okay cash-in-hand for thirty minutes staying out of the way.

Outside the Topman changing rooms I picked up some Y-fronts and a couple of flannel shirts to get us past the attendant. Thanked him on the way through, potentially a mannequin.

Drew the curtain. Getting changed in front of strangers was why I'd never learned to swim. That and watching a girl get swept away by breakers at Quay West caravan park in '96. Dad said they found her alive on Delary Beach the next day, but the newspaper boards said she died.

In my head I was mapping out the next steps of the masterplan. Told him to take everything off in as non-threatening a way as I could, and he did what I asked.

Gave him my clothes to put on, and he did that while I shaved.

The hair was trickier. I asked for some guidance and he said to get dressed first so I threw on his purple jumper and squeezed into his too tight blue jeans. Then he caught me by surprise – he gestured for me to spin around to face the mirror, and he dug his fingers into the tub and got to work on the quiff himself.

Excited – and it really was exciting now – I stood up next to him in the mirror and we swapped smiles at the uncanny resemblance.

'I better get to work.'

'Oh,' he said, and he took the lanyard off the peg on the door and put it around my neck.

'Jesus.'

He nodded. 'If…erm…if they realise, what do we say?'

I thought about it.

'We'll tell them I beat you up.'

'Okay. Or…you jumped me?'

So he knew about the shoulders…

I pulled back the curtain and the mannequin looked up in shock.

Nick said 'What about bruises?'

'If I get caught, I'll come out and give you some.' I winked at him but he didn't like the joke. 'Meet me in Patterson's,' I said. 'Ten-to-two.'

21. The Password

When I walked through the door Tuppence was two bites into a peanut butter baguette, playing with a stray hair in his Nazi fringe.

I went to the barrier, acted casual.

Picture on the card had our face worn away from the eyes up, and a biro afro where the quiff used to be. I scanned in. And it waited. And it waited. And then the arrow went green.

On the orange walls in the hallway now there were four big words stencilled in white: Lock, Up, Marco, McGann.

I looked through the door handles onto the floor. Recognised next to nobody. Empty desks were constant threats of redundancy, with cables scattered across them where PCs had been ripped out and thrown into compensation packages. Everybody looked tired. I felt pretty good.

Upstairs the row of internal windows had been baby-proofed and fogged up most of the way.

Stant's light was on, and his window – which did still open – was wide.

I pulled the door and went out onto the floor with my eyes on the carpet.

Lydia Cole was back. She was whining about call stats at a dumbbell who'd been in the job since before she was born.

The voices hummed together into a chorus, and the folks with no volume control boomed over the top like the Three Tenors hitting 'Nessun Dorma'.

Up on Bay Three Beatty blew his nose too hard on an already finished tissue. I slid onto the chair in front of Sarah's old desk – Nick's desk – pulled the lever to drop it down and hide behind the monitor.

As far as I could tell I'd gone unnoticed, helped by the fact that eye contact at Rhoder & Dalt was a sanctionable offence.

The time was projected in red onto a ten-foot window blind that never got opened. It was one-twenty-nine. I switched Nick's phone from Lunch to Personal – setting they used to measure your toilet breaks.

The login screen waited for me. Dared me to try my old details and set off Stant's panic alarm.

Then first there was a smattering of this awful applause from Bay Two, and after that something else – someone breathing hard – grunting – pounding around the pillars, coming towards me. The Meathead.

I listened for him in the hum, and I turned as slowly as I could, holding the breeziest expression I had in me, and he saw me do it. And he came for me like I was waving a red rag, and I pulled on the headset in front of me and put my face down to the keys, and I braced, and I smelled his bolognese sweat and the kids' deodorant he spiced it with, but it didn't stop. It wafted past, and I looked up and watched him start running, and I watched him almost run into the women's toilets then realise and make the men's.

Personal time was no more than ten minutes a day, no more than thirty a week. Number one frowned upon, number two out of the question.

Anyway, Plan A was to get into Sarah's account, which, as long as IT was still Henrik the Swedish alcoholic, would still be active on the system when hell froze over.

Clock on the blind flicked to one-thirty at exactly the same time as the one on the screen. In twenty minutes there was going to be a guy dressed as me outside getting pretty nervous, and in less than that Beatty would be onto me to take some calls.

I sat up, put SaltSa in the username box.

Three password strikes and you had to call Henrik.

Calling Henrik to do an impersonation of Sarah in the hope nobody told him she'd left was the kind of Plan B you didn't ever want to go public. But guessing passwords is harder than you'd think.

'Hi, is that Henrik?'

'Schpeaking.'

'It's uh… Sarah. Sarah Salt. Up on the service floor.'

'Can you schpeak up, I can't hear you.'

Key thing about bad impersonations is keep the volume down and the sentences short. I pushed the mic against my top lip.

'S-a-r-a-h S-a-l-t.'

'Okay Shara, what's the problem please?'

'I've locked myself out of my account.'

'You'll have to schpeak a bit louder please.'

Flaky top of Beatty's scalp was twitching restlessly across from me. I put my head down to the desk, turned it up a notch.

'I've been locked out of my computer.'

'Okay, one second.' Tapped away. 'Okay Shara, I just need to ask you a security question.'

Fuck.

'Go ahead.'

'What was the name of your childhood hero?'

Looked up at the blind, couldn't tell if I was sweating or some of the hair stuff had bled onto my forehead. Both.

I mean what kind of a question was that? How was I supposed to know? Even if I did know all of her heroes, what did childhood mean? Three? Fifteen?

Plucked a keyboard sanitiser wipe out of a dispenser tube, dabbed my face. And I was weighing up whether to go for The Little Mermaid or Sylvia Plath when Henrik got bored of waiting, threw me a lifeline.

'Or what colour was your first car?'

She never had a car. Syn was her first car.

'Syn.'

'Sorry?'

'Oh shit – red. Red car.'

Totally dropped the voice. Henrik didn't care, wanted me off the phone.

'Okay Shara, I've got your password here. Looks like you last changed it six months ago?'

Even under Mick you were meant to change your password every couple of hours in case you told your family and they decided to come in and send a till unit to Marks and Spencer.

'I've been off ill. Dysentery.'

'I'll give you the password, and the system will prompt you to add a new one, okay?'

Airtight.

'Great.'

'When you're ready?'

'Fire away.'
'M.'
'M.'
'A.'
'A.'
'R.'
'R.'
'C.'
'C.'
'O.'
'Marco?'
'Yes, with the question mark at the end.'

I watched the letters morph into bullet point dots, and in my periphery the minutes on the blind ticked again. And I had this strange reluctance to touch Enter. This feeling of doors closing me into a dark corridor.

'Has it asked you for a new password?'

'Uh, yes.'

'Good luck, Miss Salt.'

He hung up, and I pulled the skin on my knee as hard as I could.

I wrote *Oneforsorrow?*, let the blue wheel hypnotise me.

One-thirty-three.

One-thirty-four. Shoddy clogged system we packaged up and sold on as state of the art.

I blinked, looked around to see if the Meathead had resurfaced. Reckoned I had the beating of him across the ground, but I'd been caught by magnetic doors before.

Took another keyboard wipe, put it over my fingernails and scraped across my forehead.

Across from me Beatty blew his nose so hard my keyboard vibrated, and maybe that triggered the PC or maybe it had nothing to do with it.

On the home screen a thousand sticky notes loaded like the Nokia Snake, ate a comic strip wallpaper I didn't read in time. *Consider Weimaraner, ask mum yorkshire puddings, Eucerin, ruin Marco's life, spin class 8–9.* Sarah maybe did a fifth of what she set out to any given day. Two fifths getting ready to go and do it. Two fifths writing sticky notes.

I looked up at the offices at the top of the stairs, saw Stant's stick-figure silhouette looking down at its kingdom and hid my face with the sanitiser.

Opened Outlook. Ran my hands over the shoddy shaving job. 947 unread emails, all with red exclamation marks because urgency inflation was out of control. Bin the lot. If people wanted me they could call me, if I'd unplugged the phone they could knock, if I didn't answer they could send an email.

Typed J in contacts and he came up first. Maybe he always did but it stung regardless. Wanted to search the outbox to see how long they'd been going at it. Clicked send message instead.

Meet me outside Boots now. URGENT.
Sarah
–xxx–

When I pressed send the blind slipped to one-thirty-six.

Picked up another sanitiser to hide me from Beatty and anyone else. And I stood up and headed in the direction of the toilets, looked at the carpet, watched the clock.

'Nick,' beanpole on helium hissed at me. I looked over and he double-took, held up a hand to apologise.

By the Bay Two printer there was a chocolate cake with six birthday candles and a note to help yourself. I kept walking, kept exfoliating with the sanitiser, and I felt the pressure change, heard the click of the window above me, and turned to see the light flick off. And I timed him getting his coat, and I timed him through the hall, and I was in his head when a thick set of fingers clasped around my hips.

'Careful,' said the Meathead, and he laughed and his bitch tits quivered against my back. I didn't laugh, froze, jammed the sanitiser into an eye which stung like a cunt, and his fingers loosened, and he said 'Oop – back to work,' stepped around me and chafed off towards the stairs, where Stant stood, looking down at Sarah's desk.

He came down them fast, with a new pair of gold-trimmed brown shoes and a handbag made of grey leather.

The Meathead beat him to the door, held it for him, and Stant said something with a snarl that made him straighten his tie and brush down the front of his shirt.

Beatty stretched his neck up to see what was happening, maybe twigged Nick wasn't at his desk.

I ducked down. Lydia Cole had just put on her Japanese anime beanie hat and mittens, heading out for a vape and a second slice of that birthday cake she'd stuffed in her bra. I couldn't see Matthews. Not on the floor, not on patrol, but he never took a day off.

One-thirty-eight.

I kept the sanitiser-mask, went for the stairs Stant came down, took them three at a time, nearly lost a shoe on one but hooked it back into place. Pushed through the door.

The hallway was dark. Painted brown not orange, like a manor house with the portraits stolen and replaced with security cameras.

There was a light coming from MR1. I looked around the door. Spider plant needed a glass of water.

No life in MR2. Pulled the drawers out of a filing cabinet,

and through what was left of the window I watched the clock hit thirty-nine

Faster.

Down the hall there was the Account Managers office, and I could hear them machine gunning keyboards in otherwise silence. They were decent men, but there was no way they'd get their hands dirty with me. Everybody had kids and credit scores.

I slid along the wall.

Somewhere around there was a fly but I couldn't see it unless it hit the light in one of the doorways. He bashed himself a few times against the window on the AM office door but no-one let him in.

Slid on, ducked under the window and went around the corner to Stant's office. Pulled the handle down and it screeched and I winced. Nobody came.

Locked. I wanted to smear shit on the little brass nameplate he'd glued over Mick's – R. J. Stant, like he was President.

I'd been there a year when Mick first spoke to me. Combover, shoulderpads, varifocals. Lock up your kids.

'Martin McCann,' he said. I span around on my chair and acknowledged him, and fists on his hips he said 'Ha!' and his jaw dropped like he dislocated it when he laughed. '*Marco*, son,' he hit me in the arm, 'you're new, so I'll let you off. We're a team here. If someone's getting something wrong we tell them. Even if it's me. Okay?'

Catshit, 'Of course.'

'My door's always open.'

22. The Key

The door was never open, but when Mick was on holiday somebody had to feed the goldfish. He didn't trust Stant with that – said he was worried he'd try fucking them if he thought no-one was looking.

Mick kept the spare key in the frame of a picture of Chenery Rhoder and Tony Dalt. Rhoder looked like a shit eater and Dalt looked like he knew it.

I lifted the frame away from the wall and the key hit the carpet, and I scrambled down to ground level thinking it might have gone under the door or something, when this wheezing, slavering sound split the dark.

'Marc?' Jerry Matthews said. He was holding the key in his hand, and some folders and a lunchbox and a piece of cake with the icing licked off. I didn't know how he'd managed to get the jump on me but that was how it was. His navy suit billowed around in the breeze from the air conditioning vents. Air conditioning in the Midlands. I thought about launching at him but I didn't want any noise. Put my finger on my lip and spoke around it.

'Jerry.'

Instantly a nervous wreck, he joined in the whispering, said 'What you doin 'ere, lad?' Checked the hallway behind him. I stayed down.

'I need something from the office. Something really important.'

'E's only popped out Marc – you can't be in 'ere!'

I stood up, nice and slow like I didn't bite.

'Look, 'es very private about 'is office Marc,' he said.

'Jerry,' I said, 'what are you doing up here?'

That threw him in a weird way, and he gave his dicky knee a trademark rub down to try to disguise it.

'Aye work 'ere Marc. Es you I'm worried abou'.' The stress was making him more Welsh.

'Yeah Jerry, but I mean why are you up here? You don't work upstairs, do you?'

He was thinking about lying to me but I didn't give him time to.

I said 'They didn't *promote* you did they?'

Weak spot. Achilles heel. Dicky knee. We all know each other's – thing that keeps you up at night. We talk about it behind your back, pretend we're concerned. We reckon we've got the solution – look at us, *we've* got it *made*. Best not to get involved though. Wouldn't want to be liable if it all goes to shit.

Moved over and put my hand on his shoulder, which Nick had responded well to. Quick, forceful resolution.

I could feel the beat of the red clock in the back of my head. Gigger told me I should go to A&E if I kept getting that sensation.

Put my lips on Jerry's eardrum.

'I can hear it too.' Looked around me and he followed my eyes. 'I know you can hear it.'

'Hear wha'?'

'Shhh!'

Grabbed his face, knew he'd be too polite to cake me, pressed my ear against his forehead. Said 'He's in there…'

'What?'

'He's in there, isn't he? He's in there, pulling the strings, telling you keep your hands clean and it's only a matter of time.'

'What are you talkin' about?'

'You know what I'm talking about.'

'I promise you I don't.'

'They didn't do it when Draper died, they didn't do it when Cole disappeared.'

'Marc…'

'They're never going to do it, Jerry.' I looked serious. I was. 'He's got you in a little shoebox. No holes. No daylight. And you're never coming out.'

He looked at me like I'd broken his spirit, but I couldn't take the credit for that.

'He's got me in one too. Sarah. Everybody.'

His hair was falling out in clumps in front of me.

'If I don't get in this office right now, he's gonna get my shoebox, and he's gonna stamp on it, stamp on it, stamp on it until I'm a flat little rabbit, and then he's gonna put me in the bin. Forever.' I saw his fingers tighten on the key. 'Notice there are no cameras on his office. One place in the whole kingdom…' He tried not to look around. 'Oh Jerry… Don't say nobody told you the rumours about the Post Office?'

I moved my hand down his blazer sleeve, resolved to break his fingers, but he stopped me, straightened up and pushed me aside. And he stepped to the door and put the key in the lock, and when he turned it his arm jutted out and he lost hold of the lunchbox, and I tried to catch it but I couldn't, and the sound of it hitting the floor echoed down the hall. We stood and watched the dark. Beat. Beat. Beat. Nobody came. He opened the door, and I moved in.

It was one-forty-three on the blind. Stant could already have left Boots, spoken to Sarah, worked out he'd been hoodwinked. He could be running.

The office was cleaner than I'd ever seen it.

Mick said presentation was the key to business and Stant took it seriously. 'The façade. Game playing, son,' he said. 'The thing maybe Stanty's a little bit ahead of you in.'

Before he retired he sent the two of us to the McDonald's headquarters in London. They'd been toying with the idea of giving us a contract in the North for a decade and Mick wanted a jewel in his crown.

I drove and Stant went first-class, and he bought a three piece and I straightened a shirt out in the traffic on the North Circular.

Eight hours arguing the price of a four hour call-out, we accepted the deadlock. They wouldn't pay higher and we couldn't make our margin if we went lower. We shook hands and we all said we'd try again, and when I went to leave Stant asked who wanted to go for a drink. I had the car and I'd rather cum in my own mouth than go for beers with him, so I made my excuses.

The next day at the office Mick emailed me a photo of them all at dinner, titled it 'Persistence'. They had glasses of champagne and they were shaking Stant's hand and he had teeth up to his ears. Mick said there was a real chance of a contract.

Stant had a trophy in the cabinet. Big one. Champions League. I had a few Employee of the Weeks and a sideline feeding goldfish. The big job was drifting away.

But multinationals are slippery. A week later they backed out on a technicality and Mick was livid and I was ecstatic.

Sarah said it was an ugly idea, and she was right like always, but I printed out the picture and put it in Stant's pigeonhole.

The office was clean, but he'd taken up smoking and you could smell it on the walls. There was a sickly aftershave there too but it didn't mask it. Mick wouldn't have liked that – not with the amount of cancer in his family. He'd lost his sense of smell when he was manager of a paint factory in the eighties, but he reckoned he could always smell smoke, and he didn't respect it.

Matthews was losing his nerve already. He stood to the side of the big window and watched the doors out of it, chewing the fat in his bottom lip.

I pulled at the drawers of the desk and they struggled out past the woodswell and too much varnish. Empty, all of them, except for the bottom one where there was a bottle of good whiskey. I took it out and had a swig, offered Jerry some but he didn't want it so I had his too, and one more for the nerves and another for Diana.

Put the bottle in my pocket. Nick's pocket.

Lockers against the back wall had keys in the doors. I turned them, threw them open. Empty. Empty. Empty.

Jerry was leaning out into the hallway now, sweating so hard his suit wasn't puffing around anymore, and he was saying 'Come on, come on, come on,' like he had a rocking horse in the National.

Every drawer, every cupboard, every shelf. Empty like a model village.

The thudding came again in the back of my head. Some sort of nuclear warning system.

'Get a move on Marc!' he begged me. 'What you looking for?'

Good question. Very good question.

'I'm chasing a wild goose, Jerry. Get the fuck involved.'

'Jesus Marc!' he said. I took out the whiskey and had another swig. Offered it to him, and he took it and had one, gave it back and went to the window.

Blind said forty-six.

Started feeling around photo frames and Jerry saw that and he really started panicking, and then he said "E's 'ere! 'E's comin' Marc!' and he was right – out of the window there was Stant, angry in gold shoes, with the Meathead in step, headed for the stairs. 'Marc!' Jerry said, but I couldn't leave it. He threw the key down onto the desk and ran out of the room, and it slipped onto the floor and I snatched it up before it got away again.

I wondered if I could hide under the desk until it was just me and him, bluff the leverage and maybe have another go at butchering him if he wasn't having it.

Now my head was thudding like my brain wanted to get out, and in front of me the blue light from the computer base blinked along with the thudding, and then a green one flickered from a memory stick.

A memory stick?

I yanked it out, sniffed the end for some reason, and I jumped up and ran, put the door in the frame and locked it. Rehid the key.

They were in the hall. Stant and the muscle. Wakka wakka.

Thought I might black out from the thudding.

I went towards them. Spat on my hand and tried to slick

my hair back up but it wouldn't stay in place. The fly went for me in the dark and the buzz sent shivers.

Foot race. Head first through the two of them. Flying kick on the magnetic doors. Failing that, nice public display worthy of an insanity plea. Cut an ear off.

Gripped the corner, ready to spring. But voices… Talking… Arguing… And there was Matthews, and he was falling over himself trying to explain.

I leaned around and the shadows of Stant and his man bent over the Welshman, and in the light from the office his sweaty face was imploding, looking for answers in his lunchbox.

'You are not authorised to be up these stairs,' Stant said, and the last words hissed down the hallway. The Meathead had his arm around Matthews like he'd been in a bar fight. 'Why are you here?' I felt like Jerry could see me down the hall, like he was readying himself to throw in the towel, hand me over to them.

'It's Jonny, boss. 'E's asked me to sort some tickets for him, an' I'm on me lunch break so I tho' why not?'

I couldn't believe what I was hearing. A trick of the mind. I wanted to walk around there and kiss the fat cunt, hold him, tell him mommy made a good man.

There was silence.

'Jonny?' asked Stant. 'Well why the f—' he was trying to puzzle it together. 'Well let's go and see Jonny then, see what he's got to say.'

He brushed him aside and stormed through the door to the Account Managers, and the yellow light lit up the hallway. Matthews and the Meathead followed him.

I went. Fast and quiet, and slow past the door. And the fat men made a wall.

'Do I look like a clown?' Stant squawked from behind

it, and it took everything I had not to tell him.

Matthews turned an eye to me, and it was bloodshot red, and with the heel of his shoe he pushed the door closed, and I ran.

At the bottom of the stairs I slowed down, but only a little.

The blind said one-forty-eight. In a minute there'd be two of us.

In the orange hallway I passed Tuppence again without a word. He was walking quickly the other way, squeezing his walkie-talkie.

I scanned out.

Behind the front desk there was a live CCTV screen of the outside and the fire doors. I disconnected the external hard drive and the screens went blank, and I put it away with the memory stick and the whiskey.

For pudding Tuppence had a Crunch Corner waiting. I ate the chocolate nuggets and spooned a bit of yoghurt across his space bar.

23. The Tight Schedule

I threw the hard drive off a canal bridge before Gigger told me it might have anything important on it. Drank the whiskey.

I'd swapped clothes with Nick in the alley behind Patterson's and given him four quid and a trolley token. He was in too much of a hurry to ask me how it went but I said he was safe. I said if Beatty gave him shit to get in touch with me, but I didn't give him a number.

Gigger arrived on the back of a derestricted Peugeot Speedfight driven by some sixteen-year-old who owed him a favour. He took his helmet off and uncrumpled a spliff for me out of it, got his laptop out of a shoulder bag.

I asked him if he thought I should dive for the hard drive but he said if I came out alive it probably wouldn't work. The water was luminous green, and there was a catalogue range of pushchairs half-submerged in it plus a few of the catalogues themselves. The underside of a pigeon floated past and then bobbed down like something was sucking on its head.

I handed over the memory stick and we got in the car.

'Bit of a mess, man,' he said after a few bends, blew air up through his nostrils and put his slippers on the dashboard. 'Bloke needs a new filing system.' On the screen there were hundreds of documents with phone number titles.

If you could trust anybody to help, you could trust Tommy. At high school the careers woman told him he could do anything he wanted. He said that was a cop-out, questioned her competence, discussed her skillset, pointed her towards nursing. Tommy himself didn't believe in work, styled himself as a freelancer, refused to whore himself out so never got any commissions. He was the best though – insane recall, sorted information like poles in a Tetris matrix. In a way, that was worrying – if Tommy didn't find something to stop Stant, nobody would.

I missed a right turn, took the next one down a dead-end to make up for it.

Gigger was whistling with his tongue, playing a game of Minesweeper on one half of the screen. He said 'Hmm,' and he looked up through the windscreen for a while, and he said 'Very strange, man.'

'Strange?'

'Very.' He lit my spliff off the back of his own, told me to break the law.

24. The Check

Time was everything. I'd never ironed faster. Gigger brought his mom into it now too, and they were playing online chess and racing each other through Stant's files.

He said the nice thing about it being such a mess was that you knew there had to be a door left open somewhere. That was reassuring.

I'd had most of a bottle of whiskey and a fathead chaser, so when I looked at the spreadsheet they were working on the cells fell into each other.

'Travel expenses.' He was scratching the hair on his stomach, which was shaped like an inverted Christmas tree. 'Our friend doesn't seem to know how to put a password lock on things he edits himself, man.'

I sat down on the arm of the chair and Gigger moved the old lady into check.

'These meetings he's claimed petrol for…so, take these – eighth of December: twelve meetings at Post Office branches.'

'That's a lot of meetings.'

Idea of Mick ever leaving the office was laughable. Visiting branches absurd. Used to say something like if the lion follows the vultures, pretty soon they'll tear him apart. Guy was full of shit – internalised a shelf of management bibles and conference slides, ladled out quotes like Ghandi in a necktie.

Gigger put his thumb between his front teeth and tucked some hair behind his ear, moved her into check again.

'Mom's done the mileage, see?' I couldn't. 'Eighth of December: 540 miles. January twelfth: 600 plus, and so on.'

He turned the screen to me, scrolled all the way down to March.

'What's he doing, collecting stamps? The engineers won't do anything like these distances, never mind the boss. December eighth…with no traffic I'd say he'd make it to eight, maybe nine of these branches in a day. Never twelve. They're all over the country. Taintley's in the middle of nowhere, man – you can't get there at high tide.'

He took her castle, moved her back into check.

I stood up, tried to make sense of it, ate what was left of a Nesquik bar on the mantelpiece.

The old lady had a smile coming on. Weighing up a big move.

I said 'If he's fucking them over on expenses…maybe that's enough on its own?'

'To stop him going to court?'

'Yeah.'

'Expenses scandals are barely even scandals. Slap on the wrist stuff, man – entrepreneurial if anything. You wanna blackmail somebody, you've got to have them under a guillotine. We know he's embezzling…'

'Everyone's at it.'

'Everyone's at it, man. We need to work out how, and

we need something to prove it.' Ran his finger down the screen. 'Oldon – little one by the snail statue – January sixth.' He closed the lid before it could finish telling him he'd been checkmated, told me to put on the suit.

25. The Postmaster's Printer

Oldon was a mess of warehouses and closed down shops. The Post Office was next door to an ex-dentist and a burned-out tanning salon everybody said was an insurance job.

Gigger straightened my tie, soaked me in aftershave to cover up the booze. He said he'd wait in the car.

Old woman behind the glass was sorting banknotes like a Poker dealer with a dose of Parkinson's.

She said 'I'll be with you in a minute Jo,' to the woman in front, also shaking.

I held my hand out flat. Full house.

Jo said 'No hurry, Ruth.' Didn't consult me.

Ruth licked the tip of her thumb for every note because her skin had no oil in it.

Eventually she bent to the mic.

'Ow-kay.'

Jo stepped up, said things like 'Mia Fowler's husband died Tuesday gone,' then realised she'd forgotten her parcel, said she'd try again tomorrow.

'Ow-kay duck,' Ruth beckoned me.

I didn't say anything, just smiled and put down a Rhoder & Dalt business card I found lying around that said I was called Marcus McCann. She pulled it through the flap and started searching for her glasses, which were hanging from a chain around her neck.

Eventually she found them, propped them on the end of her nose so her eyes magnified all the way out to the frame.

'Let's see,' she said. 'Rhoder & Dalt, tech-logistics.' She took off the glasses but kept a hold of them. 'What does it mean, duck?'

'We fix your computers.'

She lifted up the glasses and looked at me, then back at the card.

'It's the printer needs fixing duck, not the computer.'

She bent down and pulled out the receipt printer from under the desk. It had seen better days.

'I'm not actually the engineer.'

'Oh.' She put it back down, lifted the glasses back to her nose. 'You're just delivering the part?'

I said 'I'm here about the money. Payment of the money.'

She looked embarrassed. 'Oh I am sorry Mr…McCann, I'm only part-time you see. Just the day-to-day. It's the Postmaster that'll know all about the money and that lot, you know. He's at the 'ospital today.'

'Shit. When's he back?'

'Not until tomorrow now. It's the rehabilitation treatment. Gang of youths almost killed him with the swings on Worley Park.'

'And you don't know anything about the payment?'

She thought about it. Her pupils looked like cigarette burns.

'I knew how to do it on the computer. On the Sunset. Cos it was all set up for you there wasn't it. But not since you've gone onto the phones. Tony's the only one who can do that.'

'You don't use Sunset anymore?' – Rhoder & Dalt's awful software.

'Well we do for the ordering, you know? Just he pays the money over the phone.'

'Over the phone?'

'Yes. That's right isn't it, cos they'll only have it from the Postmaster, he said?'

I couldn't believe what I was hearing.

'Who said?'

'Ooh I don't know duck – I don't want to tell you the wrong thing. If you haven't had the money then he might have forgotten this month's cos he doesn't remember anything from the last twenty-five years at the moment.' She was opening the till, reaching for the twenties, and I really could have had as many as I wanted but I only took a couple.

'The details of the account he pays into, would he have written them down?'

She had no idea.

'The details?'

'The numbers. Sort code. Account number.'

She pushed her glasses up her nose and started routing through little notes and scraps of paper around the desk and over on the noticeboard.

I said 'The last record we've got of a visit's January sixth, if that helps?'

When she got back to the mic she told me 'They call him – well Mr Webb, the Postmaster – you see. They call him on his mobile phone…so I don't know if he'd have it written down. He usually keeps it all in receipts if he does, but with the printer…' She held up the printer again. It was no anomaly, Rhoder & Dalt's business was fleecing employees and fiddling statistics, not fixing electrical equipment. 'And since the swings I can't make head nor tail of some of the notes he's been leaving.'

On the noticeboard there was a crayon drawing of a pig, signed Ian Webb, aged sixty-three.

I wanted to leave her alone now. The way she was diddering made me feel like a criminal.

She said 'I can leave a message for him, for when he gets back, if you like?'

'That's okay.' I said. Behind me there was a man waiting, with that really ugly kind of straight black hair and a parcel that looked like it had been taped up in a hurry. I pulled out the twenties and put them back through the flap. 'Just tell him for me: he's overpaid this quarter. If anyone calls to ask for more, he can tell them to shove it.'

She looked impressed, and lost.

'If the printer's not feeding paper, lift up the lid and under the feed button there's a screw. Get a coin that fits and screw it down. If it doesn't work, just go out and buy a new one and take it out of next quarter, and tell Stant I said that too.'

I got into Syn and swapped seats with a cloud of smoke. Gigger had a spreadsheet open – set of dates highlighted in multicolour. I turned down the spliff.

Told him Stant was calling the Postmasters on their mobiles, getting them to pay over the phone, and he nodded his head for a while, chewed it over.

'I asked for the account numbers—'

'They won't have it. And if he's got half a brain, he'll have it going into a company account only he's got access to.'

'So what then? I could get a statement from her?'

He looked down at the laptop screen. Knew something I didn't.

'My concern's if Stant gets a little scare – if we don't get him bang to rights – he buries it and buries you before anything can come out.'

'...'

'I think we've got one go at it, man. Need something stronger than a statement.'

'So what then?'

For a second he played with the door handle, looked like he wanted out.

Then he said 'Mom called. Said every Post Office in the list pops up at three month intervals.' He licked a thumb and a finger and used them to kill the spliff halfway down. 'If he's listing phone calls as meetings…that makes sense – call up every three months, get them to send the money.'

'And the expenses claims make it look like he's hands-on running the account.'

'Yeah…'

'So…'

'There's one irregularity. And it could be nothing. Could be a mistake.'

'What is it?'

He clicked to filter the spreadsheet.

'He called one branch twice in the same month.'

'Where?'

Turned the screen to face me.

'Warrester.'

26. The Second Coming

On the radio they were playing a song I liked. Didn't know the words but I sang along anyway. Hit the dash and the wheel and the windows like a drum kit. When it finished the presenter said he liked it too and then he cut off and went static because Warrester's Hell.

Gigger didn't want me to go, and he knew he wouldn't stop me. Said whatever happened he'd be at Birmingham Crown Court on Saturday, nine a.m. sharp.

'Post Office'll be closed by the time you get there.'

I told him I'd park up and wait. Only way I could relax.

'Aye, nowt better than kipping in the car, is there? Calms me right down before a big court date, man.'

I got stuck behind a tractor for maybe three miles. Pissed off a train of cars behind me not making any go at getting around it.

My dad had the traffic lights on the New Harvey Road timed. If he got it right, he'd hit nineteen greens in a row, make the school gates on the last ring of the bell. He was the king of speed, efficiency – a real genius. Like those pathetic kids with superstar parents, I thought I had the gift too – spent my whole life racing rabbits like it got me anywhere faster. I wasn't like my dad. When I rushed, I made mistakes. Any mistake now was terminal.

I stayed behind the tractor, waved cars around me when I knew someone was coming and we all had a good laugh about it.

This time I'd turn the key slowly. Tease the music out. Tighten the coil.

The flowers on the roundabout were gone, slabbed over and replaced with a black and white sign that didn't say please.

After a while daydreaming in the junction I went left, took the bypass down to the river.

It was cold because there weren't any clouds. Parking overnight cost three-sixty. That really killed me but the cameras looked like they worked so I put the money in.

There was one other vehicle in the lot – a camper-van. I never saw who was in there, but the main light stayed on the whole time and sometimes there was a laughter track coming out of a TV set.

Around seven I went and got some chips and a cheese and onion pie.

I walked back along the front of the restaurants, and I stood in the window of La Marea and watched it for a while. It was pretty full of couples and families, and every once in a while a stream of them left and another came in and took their table. In the window I reckoned I looked pretty smart in my suit. The kid's hair glue didn't hold it up, but it kept it over to one side and that was okay.

After that I went down and found a bench by the river. The plaque said: *To Maureen, who loved this place.* On the bank on the other side there was a spiked fence with what was left of a blue carrier bag impaled on it, vibrating against the wind.

And I watched the night drivers swish over the arches of the Warrester Road Bridge, and I thought about tomorrow.

27. The First Day of Spring

Sun called in sick again. Heavy night. I slept on the back seats with my legs straddling the handbrake.

Around me people got out of their cars and children complained already that Warrester was shit, which it was.

I sat up and blinked until I could see. The camper was gone.

In the dashboard I had a toothbrush and some whitening toothpaste Gigger bought me, so I pulled it out and went at it on the back seats. When I was done I wound down a window and spat across a Mazda's petrol flap, wound up.

Needed breakfast. Milkshake maybe. Clicked my spine into place, tucked my legs in and rolled out onto the asphalt, into the personal space of a PhD in a blue hi-vis and a Fisher-Price hat. He put another couple of feet between us, didn't look at me. Looked through the windscreen at the pay and display ticket on the dashboard and shook his head.

'There an issue?' I said.

No response.

'It's—'

Your guess is as good as mine: I put my hand on his shoulder, trying to point out the ticket, and he looks like he's seen a ghost, scrambles backwards, and he's saying 'Do not assault me!' and everyone in the car park's stopped to watch the show, and one kid's got his phone out, and then we're in this freeze, like when your hand lets go of a glass and before it hits the floor.

'A manhunt is underway tonight, following what Police have called 'a devastating series of violent assaults,' triggered by the innocent actions of a young parking attendant who was 'just trying to do his job."

'Assault? What are you talking about?'

'Sir, I can't carry on this conversation if you're going to continue to make me feel physically threatened.' It was like everyone was reading rehearsal scripts for court cases against me.

'Look, okay? Relax. Relax.'

'Disturbing footage seen by Midlands Today appears to show a man in his early thirties stamping on the testicles of the parking attendant, before turning on the cameraman himself – a child with severe disabilities.'

I needed to not be on the news. Needed to not get arrested for assault the day before my assault trial. Needed to get some breakfast and get back to stopping Stant.

'I'm not being threatening, okay? I just saw you looking at my car. I saw you looking in the window, and I just wanted to show you – I have a ticket. You might have missed it, but I've got a ticket just there down on the dashboard. It says on it eighteen twenty-three. Six twenty-three this evening: the twentieth of…March.' He didn't look down at the ticket. I said 'So if your scanner isn't scanning it properly, maybe it isn't working.'

Above his head a magpie hovered as if to land on a camera, then changed its mind.

'I can have a look at it if you like – I used to work with these old things.' I gestured for him to pass it over.

'Sir,' he said, 'there's no problem with the scanner.'

'I'm just saying, this is a valid ticket. A ticket I bought last night, and if you'll just scan it again or let me scan it again, then we can work out why it isn't working.'

'Sir, I am trying to explain to you what is happening here, but I am asking you to not be aggressive when I have explained this to you.'

I agreed provisionally.

'This policy is not my own personal policy, it is the policy of Francis Grant Parking Associates, and is enforceable by a law of contract.' Spoke like they had him bugged. 'Sir, that ticket displayed in your window is indeed a ticket which lasts for twenty-four hours.'

'Uhu.'

'But unfortunately, that special offer is only available Monday to Thursday, as clearly displayed on our many signs.'

Me and the crowd panned up to the signs, and the kid filming zoomed in for my reaction. In a fat yellow box underneath everything else, it said: *24-hour special offer weekdays only*.

I looked down the lens.

'Friday's a weekday. You're joking? Friday's a weekday.' He flinched. 'And I bought the ticket last night – Thursday night.'

'If you look beneath the yellow box, you'll see a notice written in black which states unequivocally that Friday is, as far as this policy is concerned, to be considered a part of the weekend, and further to that, any ticket bought on a Thursday will cease to be in effect at the turn of midnight.'

'The parking attendant – twenty-five year old Benjamin Cunt, a PhD graduate from Birmingham University – was believed to be in a stable condition in the Queen Elisabeth hospital, when the assailant, who had escaped police custody, gained access to his ward, and once again concentrated his brutal assault on the genitals of the young academic, before fleeing into the night.'

I looked at him, and I looked through the crowd at their expectant faces.
 Jesus in the car park. Devil with a forty-pound fine machine and puppy dog eyes. Crowd of freaks baying for blood and salvation. I was being tested. This was a test.
 I took out a cigarette, lit it, and took a nice long drag. Then I opened the door, slid across and started the car. Without me asking, the crowd split apart to make a path, and when they did, I took it.

28. The Man In the Long White Coat

I took the bypass up to Bank View.

Outside number six there was a sign. Said it was sold. The windows were boarded with metal sheets and the fence over at the side was lined with barbed wire.

I put the car in front of it and stood on the driveway thinking.

'You the new kid on the block then?' Middle-aged guy in green trousers and a white coat and sunglasses.

'Who's asking?'

'Number nine. Ice-cream van.'

He stood with his hands in his coat pockets, chewing on a wooden lolly stick. On his drive there was a rusted up ice cream van that said Pirlo and Son across the front.

'No, I'm an old friend of the last owner.'

He took the stick out of his mouth and ran his front teeth through the chocolate left on it.

'Came and boarded it up a few months ago, your friend. Some trouble with the Rottweiler – wheeled him out in the compost bin.'

I raised an eyebrow.

'Only saw him very rarely. When he came to get the post. Didn't talk much. Haven't you got a number?'

'No answer,' I said.

We stood looking at it, and before he left, he said 'Seemed a bit of a prick to me.'

I walked into town.

29. The Smoking Gun

The window of Jenny's News was painted in white swirls and there was a crying face scratched into it. Jenny's name was gone too but you could see the stain of it on the bricks.

The Nisa was all the way at the other end of the high street and I was feeling faint because by now Gigger would have fed me twice, so I went into Sainsbury's. They didn't have bran without raisins and raisins gave me the trots so I bought some overpriced granola. I got blue milk too, as a treat, and I squatted outside and ate it out of the bag.

When I was finished I crossed over and gave the leftovers to a homeless guy sitting by the church. He let me use some of his water to fix my hair, told me nothing ever came free.

Nisa's windows were covered in the kind of grime you get on a shower curtain. I went in.

Like before there was no one on the front desk — just a sign that said the card machine was broken, to use the cash machine outside Sainsbury's and maybe go in there instead.

The shelves and the fridge all had these intense spotlights

on them like they were proud of how little stock they had.

In the Post Office at the back the blind was down. I knocked the glass and waited.

A TV was playing in the corner behind me. England were losing at cricket. It was on a scam box so the commentary was in another language but they didn't seem too enthusiastic about the game.

I knocked again. Called out.

When I turned back to the TV it was on the music channel. I looked around for who had the remote but I was still the only one there.

Next to the coffee machine there was a parcel-hatch. I lifted it a couple of inches, called through again, waited.

Cricket flicked back on.

There was a latch on the other side of the glass that you could only undo if the hatch was all the way down, and you were on the inside. I called out again, and when nobody came I threw the thing up so hard it snapped the latch clean off, and I slid the hatch open until it wedged in place.

Like always I went head first, took some skin off my hip, screwed the landing. There was a roll of bubble wrap to break my fall but I missed that.

Even with the hatch open there was no light. I swung an arm for the chord, pulled the blind up just far enough for a beam from the shop to get in. Moody.

Around me on the floor hundreds of envelopes had been torn open and discarded. Drug bust – Thatchers the kingpins. That or Stant had beaten me to the punch…

It didn't feel like he had. The rest of the room was pristine, stacked to the ceiling with old notebooks, diaries, wedged together like some gothic library. Somewhere in here, hidden away, there was the key.

I got the torch light on my phone, got looking through

the gold years on the diary spines.

In the shop MTV was on again. A twelve-year-old was grinding through a duet with the corpse of Robbie Williams.

And now there was a breeze trying to get the front door open, and it didn't have the conviction to do it but it did enough to flutter around some greeting cards on the desk. And I was turning the torch on them when the door to the back room flew out.

I hit the floor, ducked under the desk, and a card followed me down so I pulled that in too.

Neither of us made a sound, but we could feel each other in the room. I crushed my shins into my chest. Waited. The door they opened was letting the air all the way through the shop now, and up above me the cards were falling flat and around me the envelopes were trying to take off.

In one of my wisdom teeth there was a granola filling. I went for it with my tongue but I couldn't get the right purchase.

We waited, and then it seemed as if they went to leave but as they did another card fell, and this one came off the desk, and they stopped.

'Phyllis?' he said.

I stayed where I was. There was silver lettering on the front of the card, but I couldn't make it out.

His knees clicked a few times and then he was next to me, and he came down slow, and I looked into the space between his glasses and his eyes, and at the outline of his moustache.

He had small hands, and they fumbled slightly with the corner of the card when he tried to peel it up from the carpet. Then he sat down, and he crossed his legs, and I realised he didn't know I was there. He wasn't looking at me, and he wasn't really looking at the card either.

Sitting next to him, watching through the dark, was a shameful intrusion on a private moment, but I was pretty sure revealing myself would kill him. I breathed slowly. Closed my eyes. And the wind slammed the door like a gunshot, and it got us both, and Thatcher spun his neck around.

'Phyllis?' he said.

Nobody came. He took a while there, thinking, and then eventually he went to leave. When he reached the door I followed him up, and the card I'd had on me flopped down onto the floor, and I stopped.

He stood with his back to me, his overlong dressing gown draped across the envelope carpet between us.

'Mr Thatcher,' I said.

Still didn't turn.

'I'm afraid this branch is closed for the time being. There's another one down in Quinton Village, next to Kathy's chip shop,' he said.

'I went – they didn't have any second-class stamps. Sent me up here.'

His head bowed slightly and he stuck out his right arm towards the lightswitch, pressed it. The card at my feet had a spray of pale flowers across the front of it, said: *With Deepest Sympathy*. On the desk and on every surface around us there were more. Maybe a thousand.

At the back his hair was matted around a bald patch, and when he turned around I saw it was coming out there too. Under his nostrils there were little patches of dry skin.

I knew he recognised me somehow because of the way he blinked.

'You're the boy after the Jaguar.' I didn't say anything. 'December eighth.'

Rain Man, 1988. Best Film, Best Actor, Best Script... one other I forget.

He adjusted his glasses and they made the same sound as his knees.

I bent down and picked up the card at my feet, opened it and read the start of the note inside. Thatcher stepped over to the desk looking like he planned on doing something, then didn't.

He said 'They send plenty of cards, you know, but there haven't been many visits.' Then he opened the till and took out some change, and unlocked the parcel-hatch door and went out.

When he came back he was holding two plastic cups of coffee, and he handed one to me and shut us in. Didn't seem to notice the broken latch.

Coffee tasted like the inside of an office microwave.

'Come on,' he said, turning his back on me again and going off towards the back room. 'I don't feel like being in here just yet.'

I followed. First through a hallway with a yellower fridge than mine, then into a sweaty living room with a fold-out sofa pointed at a tube TV set.

Against the far wall there was a pyramid almost the size of Thatcher himself, made out of Pot Noodles.

He rolled over a swivel chair for me, and after he tucked some boxer shorts under a cushion he took the fold-out for himself.

'Now,' he started, 'maybe you can start by telling me why you're really here, Mr...'

'McGann.'

'Mr McGann.' We both had a go at our coffee. I wondered if he had any sense of taste. He gestured at my suit with his cup. 'I'd say you're dressed too well for a man who buys second-class stamps.'

'If you came close enough to smell me you might feel

differently.'

He narrowed his eyes.

The lightbulb in the room hung too low down, and the paper-sphere shade around it was full of what looked like Nerf bullet holes and dead gnats.

I took out the business card and handed it to him.

'I'm a private investigator,' I told him. 'My client's got a tight deadline and a lot to lose.'

He looked down at the card again, turned it around to see if there was something he was missing on the other side.

'So you're not Marcus McCann?'

'No.'

'And you don't work for the electrics company?'

'No I don't.'

He made a humming noise. The card was a distraction – just something satisfying about pulling it out.

Above the noodle pyramid there was a picture of the two of them at a dinner table looking maybe thirty-five. She had on a hat and plum lipstick, he wore a grey suit, and they were laughing.

I used my sleeve to dab away some of the glaze on my forehead.

'You ran the Post Office together, you and your wife?' I asked him. I could see the pain in him when he had to think about her, and I wanted to avoid inflicting that as best I could – for selfish reasons and for his sake too – but I didn't want to scare him off by being too direct, make myself look a con.

'Forty-five years,' he said, with a little pride mixed in with the sadness.

'That's a long time.'

He nodded.

'And you were across the road until…?'

'That's right, over at the – what they called The Chatterbox, see, because you went in to post a letter, and you'd be in there talking to Phyllis – or me, mind you – for… hours, sometimes.' He sat forwards like he was trying to prove he still had it in him. 'It was January two years ago, on the sixth, 2020, they shifted us over here.'

'Money saving?'

He finished his coffee and nodded at the same time, hoovered what clung to his moustache.

I asked him what he thought of the place, and he looked around himself and said it was okay when they were both there. Phyllis could make a home anywhere. In the sixties they lived in a caravan for almost a year, and they never minded.

His eyes were milky where they were white, and a dull blue where they weren't. Sometimes he looked me in mine, and sometimes he looked over my shoulder or somewhere else. He talked like I was ghosting his memoirs. That was okay with me.

I listened and tried to look interested, drank the coffee and wondered if Phyllis had taken the cafetiere with her.

'But…I'm waffling,' he said.

'Not at all.'

'You said you were in a hurry – or your client.'

'Well yes, he is.'

'Is it anyone I'd know? A local?'

Twice now he'd sucked at the brim of his empty cup.

'Not a local, no,' I said.

He hummed again.

I stopped swivelling the chair and sat up.

'Mr Thatcher, how long has your Post Office been serviced by Rhoder & Dalt Logistics?'

'The company you don't work for?'

'That's right.'

'Hmm…' He was tapping his index finger against his temple like the bottom of a Tic-Tac box. 'You know, it's hard to say because they go by so many different names these things.'

'There was a switchover in 2015, from the previous system to the current one: Sunset. That might be what you see on the screens – the orange background.'

'Well yes, I mean I do remember the pictures changing. But because we never had all of it anyway here, we didn't have to take so much notice.'

'You didn't have the whole package?'

'Well no, I mean we're not the most technologically savvy people you see.'

'So you had a different arrangement?'

'That's right,' he nodded. He was trying to work out where I was going. 'Since they brought in all those internet systems, Phyllis told them no – not in Warrester. We talked to people here. She didn't want to be sat at a box unless it had Snooker on it.'

Here was a guy who loved feeling useful, loved helping people out for nothing at all.

He said 'At heart, we always wanted it to be a Post Office. For sending letters and parcels – no car insurance or things like that.' For the first time, he was smiling. 'And they probably thought we'd be retiring soon enough anyway.'

Things were going well – I had him relaxed, friendly, vulnerable. I had to make a move, but money was different. When you talked about money the English reflex kicked in: shy away and shut down the conversation. I had to be careful.

I stood up and went over to the noodle pyramid. Inspected it like some modern art exhibit. *Loneliness*, Alan Thatcher, 2022.

Eventually I turned back to him.

'When you got Sunset – the orange background on the computer,' he was nodding at me, 'was the Sunset Direct Pay system set up too?'

He combed his moustache with his overlong fingernails while he thought about it.

'It might be on there, if I remember it rightly, but we never used it son.'

'Never?'

'Well no, you see they wanted us to – to be doing it all online – but Phyllis wouldn't have it. For forty-five years, whether they'd tried to send a man around to collect it, or get it over the phone or on the internet, she wouldn't have it. We were a Post Office. We sent our fees in the post.'

'You send your fees in the post?'

'It's the only way to get around the fraudsters. There's a lot of history of it in the industry – old dears being carted off to court, accused of pocketing company money, when it's these con men, or these hackers, you see.'

So they'd have you to think.

'So…you post it direct to their headquarters?'

He stopped combing.

'Hmm. Well I…I don't think we do actually. I'm just trying to think.'

I tried to look easy.

He said 'We did to begin with. To the city centre, I think. And then I think it changed a couple of times actually.'

Felt myself starting to urinate.

'There was a phone call a while back. Phyllis took it, you see, so it must have been…a decent way back. A young man, she said.'

'What did he say?'

'Wasn't very…polite, this young man.'

He stood up frowning at me, and he wagged his finger, and he told me to hold on a minute and then he disappeared towards the office.

He came back in and the air from the hallway felt good against the mask of sweat I had on. In his hands there was a red notebook.

'Funny this,' he said, frowned up at me with entirely justified suspicion. 'The call came in just the day after we saw you last.'

He passed it over. The old lady's writing looked like a heartbeat monitor.

Phyllis – 9/12/21.
Caller: Robert James – General Manager at Rhoder & Dalt

R.J. Stant. Like he was President. Robert James Stant.

Robert has called to say that we are no longer to send the electricals payments to 6 Bank View.

I read it again.

And again.

> *Robert says that we will be informed of a new P.O. Box address shortly, but for this quarter's payment we should post to a temporary address: 14 Quaypier Close, Warrester, West Midlands, WM8 8NF.*

> *I have informed Robert that, as has always been the case, we do not do business over the phone – that we require a signed, headed letter detailing the above, in order for the legals.*

'And that's when he did get quite rude, you see – I remember her saying. He said he didn't have time to do stupid things like that. But Phyllis said it was the second time they'd changed it in a matter of months – she was very insistent.'

From the pocket of his dressing gown he slid out a second document, printed on eggshell white paper, with a claret and blue truck at the top of it, driven by a featureless man.

30. The Piggy Bank

'You're not gonna believe it.'

'Hang on, let me…okay, go on.'

'The place with the dog.'

'The dead dog, man.'

'Who owns it?'

'Jim Stant.'

'…'

'…'

'How the fuck did you know that?'

'How did you *not* know that?'

'…'

'You told me that was where you found the ring box and the note from Sarah's dad. Who else's house was it gonna be?'

'…'

I took it off speakerphone. Thatcher sat pretending he hadn't heard, disassembling the TV remote with a screwdriver.

Gigger said 'Well anyway, how is it you've come upon that information?'

'Warrester Post Office. Stant had them sending money to the dog house.'

'Dog house is the piggy bank.'

'Or it *was*, until someone broke in and killed his dog.' Thatcher glanced over. I stepped out into the hall. 'Sells the house, calls this place and sends them a fucking signed letter saying send the money to…fourteen, Quaypier Close, Warrester.'

He thought about it.

'Where are you now?'

'Having a Pot Noodle with the Postmaster.'

'I'll get the train to Newley Parkway, grab me in an hour and we'll go together.'

I thought about it.

'I don't think so.'

'…'

'I think…' Couldn't put it into words.

'Yeah. Okay…' He called out to his mom that he'd be there in a second. Said 'Make a photocopy.'

'Okay, will do.'

'And don't expect him to take it well.'

'Okay.'

'You know where I am, man.'

'Yeah… Yeah.'

That was the last time I ever spoke to Tommy.

31. The Map

At the hatch I told Thatcher I was sorry about the broken latch and his dead wife.

Outside I closed my eyes and took in some air, let the wind cool me down.

Down by the church there was a man ringing a bell, shouting. A ring of figures in different coloured fluorescent jackets stood around him, and I wondered if any of them were police. I put up the lapels on my jacket, crossed the high street and went uphill.

I was blowing hard when I got to the Magpies. Banked on it having free Wi-Fi but the blackboard outside just said: *No kids.*

The thickest of the cloud had burned away and you could maybe believe it was spring. I sat on the wall at the front for a few minutes, plucked wings off the butterflies in my stomach and looked across the roofs, listened for the bell in the distance.

'Oi Marco.' Voice like the first bite of an apple.

I looked over my shoulder and she smiled at me with the kind of white tooth red lipstick combination they sold wars with. Amber.

'You gonna say hello or what?' she said.

'I was thinking about it.'

'One of the great thinkers of our generation.' She came over to play, sat down next to me in a blue and white striped vest and her purple jeans and red Reeboks.

'Want some?' Offered me a vape.

Shook my head. Giving up smoking was a young man's game.

Black Labrador with a piece of rope for a lead dragging behind it walked by. No owners.

She breathed out blueberry bubblegum.

'So…how you been?'

I gave her a bent smile.

'Dyou have Wi-Fi?'

Bruce's coat and a brown fedora hat were hanging by the door, but he wasn't in his seat. A full stout and a newspaper looked sick of waiting.

I asked her if I should take my socks off and she threw me a look with a big underbite and cross-eyes.

My stool at the bar was free like all the others. I drank a bottle of fruit cider, weighed up whether urinal cakes that smelled this strong were any better than piss. She had gin and Lilt. Every time she put the glass down there was a thicker coat of red around the rim.

They didn't play music, which I liked. She said there was a jukebox in the old days, but they were losing money on it. I asked how. She said she didn't know for sure and she got me out another bottle.

Same story with the Wi-Fi, so she gave me her phone, set up Maps and I searched Quaypier Close, started tracing a route.

I had it in my head we'd go through what happened last time, but in the end it never came up.

She said it was her dad's birthday. Made him a CD every year to play on his way into work. Said he didn't want anything else.

'I could make you a CD.'

I laughed. Syn didn't have a CD player and I didn't have a job.

'Oh?' she said. She was working me over but that was okay.

Stant's real estate was a mile out of town. One straight road, but I made some pretty detailed drawings of landmarks along the way because I liked the conversation.

'I used to work in logistics. Electricals.'

'But you left?'

'Artistic differences.'

She rolled those big brown eyes and I crumbled like cheap plaster.

I said 'Cutbacks, redundancies.'

Took a look up at her. I was the man at the bar telling them how it all went wrong.

'I got overlooked for a promotion and the boss kidnapped my girlfriend.'

'Jesus, what?'

'Consensually.'

She thought about how it all fitted together, cracked another Lilt.

Bruce was back at his table, tearing up a beermat. I admired the guy. He drank his stout like a hot stray, looked over the brim at me.

'So what brings you back to Warrester?' Amber asked me so I'd stop being confrontational.

I blew a whistle across the top of my bottle.

'Unfinished business.'

Now she raised up an eyebrow and let it sink back.

'Unfinished business requiring a map to somebody's house...' She was spraying the bar and wiping it over, and she signalled for me to lift up my bottle and I did. 'Lucky we were still here.'

'Was I?'

'Closes next week. Gonna blow it up, build some apartments.'

'You think Bruce'll notice?'

We both looked over at him, and she slapped me on the knuckles, went on wiping. Maybe I smiled.

'You'd be funny if you weren't such a sulk.'

I finished a sketch of a tennis club, tucked it in with the letter.

Two old dogs came in for a game of pool. I watched them play. They weren't any good. I hadn't played in years but I'd spank these two left handed.

My phone vibrated, and I let it ring out. Finished my drink and asked for a double whisky, and she smiled at me in the mirror while she poured it. I told her leave the bottle but she said they couldn't do that.

A few hours in she asked if I was having second thoughts.

I took a piss with my head propped against a sign about cancer, and I thought about asking to see her again.

Back in the bar she was pouring Bruce another creamy one. She watched me cross the room, held up a finger to say wait a minute, but I couldn't.

32. The Mansion

In the not too distance the 'Three Blind Mice' music was playing, and I wondered if there used to be a better variation in ice cream jingles.

Five missed calls on my phone. One Gigger, four Dad. I turned it off in case the court asked for my GPS records or something, jogged uphill for thirty seconds, sat in a bus stop for five minutes to recover. Gone a bit overboard on the booze.

Hearse crept by looking for a fare.

When I stood up I had a chalky smear of birdshit down the side of my trousers. They laughed at me from the trees. You had to hand it to them.

Gravity Avenue turned up between two rows of eight-foot hollybushes. It curved around willows and sycamore trees with treehouses bigger than my apartment.

At Quaypier I stopped. On either side of the junction there were these huge black gates, like nightclub security with better social skills, and under the sign there was another one that said: *Private Road – No Turning*.

I went in.

Here there were no treehouses. In front of every porch there was a manicured strip of grass to make the driveway look pretty, and a tree with sanded-down branches birds couldn't nest in.

Fourteen was at the deep end of the cul-de-sac. Two floors, but fat like a clubhouse, wrapped in those wooden slats they built US suburbs with. Turquoise. Paint flaking off and bubbling, wood warping out of place. Everybody knows don't trust a newbuild.

Still, this place had it all – huge bay windows, satellite dish, hanging baskets. Stant had a mansion, Bank View, the Jag, gold trimmed shoes, Sarah. If it wasn't my soul he'd sold I'd have seen the funny side.

Where was the Jag? Rest of the road was a luxury car showroom, and Stant wasn't the modest sort. Made me uneasy, like maybe Matthews spilled the beans about the office break-in, spooked him again and he'd gone into hiding.

I took the path to the front door in a pretty straight line, felt the neighbourhood-watch zoom in.

There was a bell, but I hit the letter flap.

Nobody came.

Sound like a baby's rattle set me on edge.

Hit it again.

Nothing.

Magpie was on the garden gate, which was eight feet high like everything else, flanked by plastic flowerbeds. He held tight, double dared me.

Foot of the gate there was a stack of yellow bricks tied up in string like a bad birthday present. I stepped up, heard a little stitching rip. Magpie shuffled over, shut the fuck up, didn't fly.

Scanned the garden. Sundial and wooden archways wrapped in ugly plastic flowers. Landscape gardener sculpted out of plastic hedge scratching his head at what to do with a watering can.

And in the greenhouse a dark figure, hidden by tomato vines and dirty glass: Sarah. Unmistakably Sarah.

She slid open the door and I ducked down, threw up a Bell's and swallowed it back.

'Are you staying there?' she said.

Didn't speak. Didn't move.

'Come on, Mr.'

This weird, musical tone I'd never heard her use. Something childlike, but maybe in that horror film kind of way where if I looked at her I'd turn to stone and they'd keep me in the garden with the hedge guy, hook me up as one of those pissing fountains.

'I've got... Fishies,' she said.

Fishies? I straightened up. She was sitting in a white patio chair facing the greenhouse, rolling a cigarette, and on the lawn in front of her a blue-grey kitten tilted its head like it wasn't exactly sure either.

If the magpie ratted me out, I was going to bite his head off, and he knew that.

'Whaaat?' she asked the kitten, and it mewed and trotted over to her, stroked itself against the hand she was smoking with, and she plucked it up onto her lap and rubbed its chin with a diamond ring.

She tickled its stomach, and she cleaned sleep out of its eyes, and called it a mucky pup. And when birds came by to taste the plastic berries she held the kitten up, told it what kind they were because that was something she always did. When they flew away she used the kitten's paw to wave them off, and then she'd roll another cigarette, smoke it all the way down to the filter.

I watched them for a while, tried to think of something funny to say, but I didn't find it funny and neither would she.

Lowered myself down, sat on the stack, tried not to be sick down my suit.

Wandered if I kidnapped the pair of them I could stop Stant going to court that way, maybe see how much I could swindle out of him and her dad at the same time.

Then finally the hum started up. Magpie turned to watch.

Quiet at first. Getting louder. Getting closer. Like a plane falling out of the sky.

'I can hear him,' Sarah said. 'He's gonna get you!'

And I thought we'd see about that.

33. The Black Cloud

When the Jag hit the junction of Gravity and Quaypier I was already there.

He rolled to a stop, and I took the envelope with the letter in out of my pocket, held it out. Pointed to it. Waved it around.

I said 'You wanna do it somewhere else, or you wanna do it in front of her?' Couldn't tell if I slurred it too much, couldn't see his face because of the light on the windscreen.

Stant thought about it, and if he was anything like me he thought about putting the car through my knees, slip it in reverse to finish the job, chop me up and mix me in with the Fishies, which were some sort of cat biscuit.

The passenger door clicked open.

'Kitten's dead,' I said, bunched the velvet blue jacket he'd left on the seat into a ball and threw it in the footwell. 'Hung it in the greenhouse.'

Nothing. Looked straight ahead.

'He took it well – did you proud.'

I clicked around the radio settings, turned up a bit of classical and Stant switched it off with some button on the wheel. He was tired, pale, brown under the eye.

I said 'La Marea? Or surprise me.'

He checked the mirrors, bent it around the junction and we headed back the way he came. Juggled the options through his head and pretended to focus on the road.

I dropped my window a few fingers to let out the sickly sweet of the aftershave he took baths in.

At the main road he turned left, away from town.

'No knife?' I asked, snapped open the glove box and flicked through a few greatest hits compilations you couldn't argue with.

Took another left without indicating. Told you everything about him you already knew.

I pulled down the visor. No knife. Pulled down his and he swerved a little, throwing it back up. Leaned over to look in his door panel. Empty Diet Coke bottle, pack of Wrigley's chewing gum. Thought about asking for one.

Blue sign said we were heading for the M-something-something, and I locked my door in case he tried bouncing me at seventy.

I could see a ball of lint in his belly button through a bulge in his shirt, and I wondered if it was a blouse because mine buttoned the opposite way. Or if mine was a blouse.

'Where we going?' Definitely slurred that one.

Sloppy Dan's was a fifties diner with a nineties Pizza Hut roof and futuristic prices. I got out first and ran in for a piss, told Stant I'd have a chocolate milkshake, and when I came out it was sitting in a window booth with him and a black coffee, lit up by the sun, who'd made it in for the last hour.

'You stink of booze,' I said, sat down, took the straw out and put away half a pint. Good as it gets. Delicious.

He was watching the Jag out of the window, and when he turned to look at me, take a sip of coffee, I thought I was having some pissed hallucination.

I said 'What happened to your face?' and it seemed like he might throw himself across the table, but instead he just asked

'What's in the envelope?'

The right side of his face, from his eye all the way down to the sharp of his jaw, was stained three shades of pink, crinkled like an old piece of fruit. Figured he was sensitive about it – he'd looked bad to begin with. Wondered if it was something I could catch, leaned back a few degrees.

'There's a copy of this.' I took it out, put it between us. 'In case you…you know.'

It was pretty hard to read what was left of his face. Always had been, on account of it being so dull and ugly, but now half of it was completely devoid of any expression.

He took the letter out, and I signalled to the waitress for another milkshake. She said she didn't work there, which didn't reflect well on the place.

'What dyou think this is?'

'What do I think it is?' I said.

He put it down, moved his coffee aside. Said 'What do you *believe* this is?'

Always did that. Patronising emphasis.

'Fuck you. I know what it is. So do you.'

'So tell me.'

'You think cos I've had a couple of pints I don't know what it is?'

'Then tell me what it is, Marco.'

Tried to summon Gigger. Reassuring, assured Gigger.

'Embezzlement.' Unintelligible.

'*Embezzlement?*'

'That's what I said.'

More milkshake. Possible chocolate moustache. Gave it a quick wipe and made a note to check in the intermission.

He said 'You think I've been embezzling money from the Post Office, by getting people to send cash to my *home address*?'

I said 'I *know* you've been…doing that.'

'And what, you think you're gonna stop me turning up tomorrow by *blackmailing* me?' He picked the letter up. 'How did you even get this? Did you think you were a little *detective*? It's standard procedure, you pathetic mess.'

Family two booths behind Stant had a quick one, looked satisfied with his appraisal, went back to their Sloppy Meals.

'We'll call them,' I said.

'What?'

'We'll *call* them.'

'Call who?'

He wasn't making this easy.

'The board. Give me your phone.'

'Give you my *phone?*'

'Come on…'

He looked out of the window, checked on the car like he had a dog tied up out there, and I took the opportunity to grab another waitress. Didn't work there either.

'Will you get someone who does?'

Gave me that look.

Now Stant turned back in, and the scars on his face seemed darker. And he never raised his voice, and he never moved an inch when he said this, and that makes you uneasy, like every time you move your own hands or you blink or whatever, you're losing. I tried to keep still, but I couldn't.

He said 'You know, from the day I started, til the day you left, I *hated* myself.'

'Don't feel bad, Jim – everybody hated you.'

'Remember that *voice* you all did? Even when I was in the room, and we'd just *pretend* I didn't know.'

'Doesn't ring a bell.'

'And how no-one sat with me at lunch like I had some *disease*, or invited me for *birthdays*…'

'Oh, the birthday parties? They were wild.'

'I thought I must be a *real* cunt, and just by *coincidence* everybody noticed at once.'

'People would have noticed before.'

'You gave me the Rim Job trophies—'

'*Mr* Rim Job.'

'And you laughed with *Mick* about me, and you wiped down *keyboards* after I used them and sprayed *air* conditioner when I left the office.' He loosened the knot of his tie. 'I thought, well I must deserve it, cos everybody *laughed*, everybody found it so *funny*. Nobody said good *morning*, asked me how I *was*.'

'And you were fucking Mother Theresa—'

'But then when you *left*…it was strange. Couple of weeks where things were the *same*, and then after a while this black cloud just…went. And this *taboo* about saying hello to me in the halls, or asking me about the car or what I was doing the weekend…*disappeared*.'

I said something about rim jobs but he wasn't listening.

He said 'Took me a while to work out, and it was *Sarah* really that helped me see it, cos she was coming to the same conclusion *herself*.'

'You guys are so cute.'

'She was coming to the same *point*.'

'Was she.'

'It was *you*.'

I picked up the milkshake, finished it off.

He said '*You* were the black cloud.'

The music on the PA system cut out. Or it seemed like it did. And now everyone in the place was looking at us and I had to get some points on the board.

'Black cloud?' Repeat things. 'I've gotta come over for one of these group therapy sessions, man. Let me get it clear: you get everything in your life that's ever gone wrong…you blame it all on one cunt, and then you sacrifice them so you can fly off into the rainbow like a butterfly, yeah? That's beautiful. Really beautiful. So you sack me. Lose me my house—'

'You took *voluntary* redundancy. Said you couldn't work under a man who braided the board's crack hair with his *teeth*.'

'Oh, I spose I volunteered my girlfriend—'

'She wasn't your girlfriend. You hadn't spoken to each other for *two* months. The last time you did, you told her you'd kill her *family* if she left you.'

Couple in the car park standing watching. Lip readers.

'Oh, I'd take her word for that yeah. I bet she's told you everything has she?' I said 'Did she tell you she left a photo for me in my pigeonhole? No? Did she tell you she wanted me to come and find her because you're such an ugly cunt she'd rather risk the bloke who'll kill her family than say yes to marrying you—'

'Photo in your pigeonhole?'

'Oh, she didn't mention that?'

'Of you in Tolten?'

'…'

For the first time, he was smiling.

'You think *she* put that there?'

Nasty, angry twist of a smile.

'You thought she wanted you to *save* her? You thought half a polaroid of you looking like a prick on the beach was a cry for *help*? How *delusional* do you have to be?'

I looked at the steam coming off the coffee, thought about throwing it in his face.

He said 'One for *sorrow*? No? You don't *remember* writing that on the back of the McDonald's photo? No? Putting it in *my* pigeonhole? No, you wouldn't. Why *would* you remember it?'

I could see the little flecks of spit spraying at me in the sunlight.

'*I* put it there. Little *joke* I thought I deserved. Make me feel a bit *better* about the last five years.'

'Fuck you.'

'But you couldn't let me have one, could you? *No*. No. You had to come after me—'

'I went after Sarah.'

'It was *Sarah's* dog you murdered with garden shears?'

'Dog you left to die in the attic?'

'*Sarah's* house that she bought for *her* elderly parents you broke into?'

'House you stole by sacking me?'

His eyes were red now, and his gums were out, and I didn't like that.

He took a couple of breaths. Leaned back and looked around at everyone pretending not to notice. And he said '*Was* it *Sarah's* face you put in the fire?'

At the back of my mind in some recut memory I saw us falling around, rolling in a dustball. Plate spins towards him, and our heads hit the stone. He's got his hands around my throat, pinning me down, and then he's trying to get away and I won't let him and I slash at him with the fork, and I pull him towards the fire but the taser snaps through me.

And then we're back in the diner, and he's saying it again like he hasn't before—

'Was it *Sarah's* face you put in the fire?'

It was a lie.

And around us they sat and chewed quietly, waited for my reply.

And Stant waited for it too and so did I.

The skin on his cheek looked thin, fragile, like you could poke a finger through it.

Fake. It was fake. He did it to himself or he always looked like that or he had on some kind of plasticine mask. I wanted to pull it off, turn things back to the letter.

'Excuse me?' Seventeen-year-old waitress in a Sloppy Dan's hat and white tights. 'We were wondering if you could keep the noise down just a little bit—'

I said 'You were wondering? Oh, cos I've been wondering where the fuck you've been while I've been sitting here waiting for a milkshake refill? Or is the policy advertise it all over the windows then hide in the kitchen so no-one ever gets one?'

Good to get it off my chest. Looked like she could take it.

Stant said 'It's okay. We're leaving.'

'Oh it's okay? It's okay with *you* that I didn't get a milkshake?'

Waitress backed away, and Stant nodded at her like he was some fucking hero. When she reached the tills, he took a drink of his coffee, watched the Jag for a second, and then he leaned in to me.

'This piece of paper...whatever you think this is. If you think it stops me doing *everything* I can to put you away for as *long* as I can tomorrow…you're even more confused than she says you are.'

He slid the letter over to me, slid out of the booth and went towards the toilets, and again I played the fight out and every time the taser came too soon—

'What?'

Fat prick watching me over a box of nuggets.

I looked down at it. Words didn't stick. Signed Jim Stant.

He was bluffing. Big fucking bluff they'd dreamed up to hammer me away.

The seventeen-year-old was back. She dropped down a new milkshake. Banana now. And she was trying to spring away without me noticing.

'Sorry,' I said.

She stopped. Didn't look me in the eye. Then she nodded and skated back to safety.

He was bluffing.

I scooped the letter, took the milkshake too, and I followed Stant and they all watched me go.

Some fucking sick move, where you steal someone's life and you goad them into coming after you, and then you melt your own face and say they tortured you. Some fucking sick move this was. And tomorrow he had the payoff, with the same story and everything he practised with Sarah, and they'd believe him, and the jury was gonna believe him and everybody else was gonna believe him. Some sick fucking move.

I kicked open the door, and Stant stood waiting, with a phone to his ear and a gold knife in his free hand. Calm.

'He's here,' he said. 'He's got a knife. Send help.'

34.

My dad taught me to drive when I was sixteen, at the car park of some football fields they built a Bowlplex on. I didn't really care about driving but he'd taught his brother and maybe my mom, and it seemed like something he believed in.

He said 'It's a good skill to have. Get you out of a bind. Stop moaning and turn the ignition on you little shitbag.'

I took a right without indicating.

Wouldn't endorse drunk driving.

Came off a roundabout at about fifty-nine and hugged the bend like a flawless Scalextric.

Seats were a dream – sturdy but lightweight, and with this untouched black leather that didn't stick and it didn't slip. No cigarette burns, no ash. Maybe a hint of his aftershave, or maybe that was on the back of my hand.

The sirens were everywhere, but they were going the wrong way and they weren't going to catch me.

Jim Stant was where he belonged: in the toilet of a fake American diner, covered in banana milkshake and a mix of both our blood. As far as I knew he wasn't dead.

Nobody was going to believe he came at me with the knife, cut through my shoulder and slit my face open from my eye down to the mouth. And maybe they'd believe I blinded him with the milkshake, and he threw me through a cubicle before I got his head in the toilet and banged the lid until he fell asleep, but that part didn't do much good if the emergency operator and everyone in the diner said I started it.

I couldn't tell you who started it.

I was looking for a post box.

Went by Gravity Avenue and I thought about Sarah waiting for him to come home, and what she'd think and what she'd say about me.

On my twenty-sixth birthday she bought me a guitar. Showed me how to play 'Here Comes the Sun' by George Harrison, and I got the first few seconds right and she said I had super powers, and we jumped around in the living room at Pound Road and I knocked the guitar off the settee and broke its neck.

Past The Two Magpies.

She didn't mind. It was pretty funny.

Into Warrester and straight over the roundabout, onto the bypass, past Bank View and Syn and the houses with turrets and guard posts.

I kicked myself for never getting it fixed.

Post box showed up on the corner of the Warrester Road Bridge. I put it on the double yellows, climbed out and tried not to get blood on the envelope.

Wrote FAO: Jerry Matthews, Rhoder & Dalt, and I didn't remember the postcode so I just wrote England. Put it in the box.

And I stood and looked out across the river, with the sun dipping down into it, and I was thinking I was going to have this moment of serenity, but that never came.

I leaned on the roof of the Jag, and I was trying to get my phone back on to maybe call my dad. Wanted him to come and save me or something. But the sirens came into earshot again, and I knew I had to go.

Threw the phone in the river.

Got in the car and took a second to try and get my heart rate down — put the fight and the cunt Stant and court out of my head — and I did a pretty good job of that.

So I was really seeing things.

Things like the young mom on the bridge, pulling apart her handbag looking for the chapstick the baby was playing with.

Like the guy twenty paces behind her, in a yellow polo top and shorts, who you just knew fucked the dog when his girlfriend went out.

I let them out the way.

Clicked on the ignition, opened up the throttle and the V8 blocked out the sirens. Charge ran through me like a thousand volts in the chair. And I thought maybe I was too close, but I didn't want to kill the mood reversing.

When the wheels hit the pavement the car tore away from the road. Pinned me down. Cracked through the stone. Pirouetted through the sky in fast forwards.

And a lifeguard in a silver sheet told the fire crew the driver-side door was sealed shut when he made it in the water.

And a woman with dry lips said I just seemed to drift towards the wall.

And they sent divers, and they sent dogs along the river banks. They put up Wanted posters in the streets and in the papers. Took Gigger to the station and searched my dad's house, told him to report it if I ever tried to call him and he said they didn't know me very well.

On the day of the funeral a walker said he saw me swimming breaststroke somewhere downstream, fully clothed, with a huge bleeding cut on my face. And they sent a boat down with a fog light, and they called my name.

But they never found me.

They never found me.

Acknowledgements

Without the people below, this book would be a file on a broken Chromebook, and the stardom that it's no doubt propelled me to a distant dream. My sincere thanks.

Jessica Bell, Julia Dean-Richards, Luke Hadley, Amrit Kaur, Embolon Theatre, Ryan Mooney, Charlotte Kovac-Hutchinson, William Fisher, Olivia James, Daniel J Brian, Nick Holdaway, Stuart Smith, Michael Smith, Matilda Hartley, Ray Jacobs, Victoria Denny, Ness Dean-Richards, Ethan Dean-Richards, James Maxwell, Ann Jones, Iona May, Matt J Davenport, Andy Hill, Richard Laverick, Sarah Steventon, Dan Kovac-Hutchinson, Shaun Best, Tony Chenery, Tom Peters, Wayne Dean-Richards, Earl Richards.

About the Author

Kalman Dean-Richards is a novelist and filmmaker from the Black Country, England.